Ir

MW00945714

The Pawn on the Chessboard

TRANSLATED FROM THE FRENCH BY
Stephen Wilson

LAMAD VAV PRESS
Oxford

Lamad Vav Press, Oxford

The Pawn on the Chessboard

Translation © Stephen Wilson 2013

First published in French under the title *Le Pion sur
l'échiquier,*
© Éditions Albin Michel, 1934

ISBN 13: :978-1481077095
ISBN 10 : 1481077090

Also available as Kindle edition on Amazon.co.uk
The Child Prodigy by Irène Némirovsky
Translated from the French by Stephen Wilson

For Jacob, Esme, Saar and Seth, new lives

Translator's note

Irène Némirovsky wrote this novella in 1932-33 during the period following her father's death. It first appeared as a serial in the daily paper, *L'Intransigeant,* and was followed in 1934 by a revised version in book form. Its publication coincided with Hitler's rise to power in Germany, the establishment of the Gestapo, and the passing of a series of laws disenfranchising Jews in that country, which presaged the genocidal attack that was to follow throughout Europe. Némirovsky was born in 1903 to a wealthy Jewish banking family in Kiev, Russia (now Ukraine), but she was brought up speaking French. Her mother spoke French and she had a French governess during her formative years, whom she loved. When she was fifteen years old, her family fled the Russian revolution, eventually settling in Paris in 1919. She considered France a 'civilised country', she was educated at the Sorbonne and she wrote in the French language. But at a time when fear of being inundated with Russian Jewish immigrants ran high, she and her husband were repeatedly refused naturalisation. In 1942, she was arrested by French gendarmes and subsequently deported to Auschwitz, where she died. Her husband, Michel Epstein, was murdered there several months later.

Two children, Denise aged thirteen and Elisabeth aged five, were told to run home, grab what they could, and disappear. They survived. The text of a project their mother had been working on at the time of her death, reflecting French life under Nazi occupation, was preserved in a small suitcase, but its literary significance went unappreciated for many years. *Suite Française* was eventually published in 2004 to wide critical acclaim. The book became an immediate bestseller.

Némirovsky's early novel, *David Golder*, published in 1929, also enjoyed spectacular success and was adapted for both stage and screen. It was hailed as a masterpiece. But her depiction of Jewish characters involved in high finance, modelled on her own family experience, attracted accusations of anti-Semitism. And it is certainly true that she made use of popular anti-Semitic caricature. Albeit a picture of an emotionally impoverished family, an unloving wife and mother, manipulative daughter, and ruthless businessman father, *David Golder* is at the same time a critique of all human narcissism. It is essentially a tragedy.

The world she brought to life was the world she knew, but it was seen through the eyes of 'the other'. Her attitude toward her own background appears to have been soured not only by prevalent cultural anti-Jewish prejudice and her wish to be accepted as a 'French writer', but also by a conflicted relationship with her parents. As late as 1938, regarding her novella *Fraternité*, Némirovsky noted, "I'm certainly going to get bawled out again for speaking of Jews at this time, but bah!...". She converted to Catholicism during the same year.

A single overtly anti-Semitic reference occurs in *Le Pion sur l'échiquier* when Christophe Bohun contemptuously refers to his hated boss, Beryl, as 'a little Jew born on the outskirts of Romania'. There is nothing in the book to indicate that the Bohun family itself is Jewish. Indeed the author has chosen a name linked to Anglo-Norman aristocracy and a seventeenth century Ukrainian Cossack military leader. Yet the single-minded obsession with money, the dishonest dealings, the lack of 'humanity', the conspiracy to promote and profit from war, the blackmail, the hereditary 'taint' apparently passed down the generations, the origin in a sordid Greek port where his father was a money-lender, make James Bohun a character that answers to all the tired anti-Semitic clichés.

But in this book, Némirovsky's concern with the corruption of values is ultimately no more directed against Jews than is Shakespeare's *Timon of Athens* directed against Athenians. Despite her personal history, and perhaps unwittingly, *Le Pion sur l'échiquier* is an object lesson in Hegelian thought and Marxist sociological analysis. If she erred in portraying modernistic alienation and anomie, writ small in her Jewish or quasi-Jewish characters, it was not so much a naïve and cruelly ironic failure to see the danger of doing this in the context of her time, but an inwardly driven need to come to terms with, perhaps distance herself from, Jewish identity as she experienced it – her own and that of others, be they banker or Bolshevik. It was something she was compelled to do, despite the way it played into the hands of Nazi propaganda, and the unthinkable uses to which her art could be bent.

"After all, myself, Jews, I love them like guinea pigs!", she confided to her notebook in May 1938, words whose horrific associations in a post-Holocaust world, she could never have imagined.

***

Le Pion sur l'échiquier has lost none of its bite during the eighty years since it was written. But some of the vocabulary has fallen out of use, for example the word 'grue', literally a crane, which I have translated 'flash-tail', is no longer commonly used slang for prostitute. Similarly 'boîte à musique', clearly some kind of early 'Duke Box', worked by turning a handle, which I have translated 'music box', rather than 'musical box', is not familiar to modern readers. The term 'Negro' is now considered by many to be offensive but was in common use during the 1930's, and I have faithfully translated it from the French 'Nègre'.

Némirovsky's sentences are often long and punctuated with numerous ellipses. I have tended to preserve their structure and not striven too hard to naturalise them into smooth English. Some words, for example 'brusquement' - 'abruptly', 'à mi-voix' – 'in an undertone' or 'machinalement' – 'mechanically', occur so frequently as to be stylistically oppressive, but I have resisted the temptation to edit them, feeling that the repetitions are germane to the text. Similarly the lack of consistency in the use of speech marks has been left, despite the difficulties it inflicts upon the reader. More than likely the book was produced under pressure and hurriedly edited.

Where English words occur, for example in the lyric of a popular song, they are always in italics which I have preserved. Where French words occur that are familiar to the Anglophone reader, such as 'monsieur' or 'Allo!Allo!', I have preserved the French in order to create atmosphere. Finally, I owe many thanks to my friends, Gabriel LeFèvre, Aude Mille, and Derek Summers, and to my wife, Kate Wilson, for helpful responses to questions that I raised. Naturally, any errors in translation are mine alone.

Stephen Wilson, Oxford, November 2012

1

Finished for today, Christophe Bohun muttered
to himself, in the deep shadow of the empty
stairway.

He was rushing out of the office first, as usual,
as if it were a house on fire. But, for a short
moment, he leant against the cold wall with a
feeling of pleasure; he was moved by the darkness
and the silence; his trembling hands nervously felt
around the pockets of his coat, extracted a pack of
cigarettes, the lighter; he grabbed a cigarette with
such haste that it broke in half, threw it away, lit a
second one, greedily inhaled the smoke.

The ends of his fingers were still shaking. He
rubbed his eyelids for a long time, dazzled by the
glare of lamps, half closed his eyes, yawned, began
to go down.

One day gone by…One day less to live… And
for that, thank the gods…

The footfall of workers leaving their offices
reverberated on the steps like distant thunder. They
emerged from the shadowy stair-cage, flowing in
front of the glass roof, highlighted yellow in the
brilliant October sunset, then they were plunged
again into obscurity. The lenses of lorgnettes,
spectacles, touched by the light, threw up bright
flashes, instantly extinguished. Below, the gas
lamps hissed. The building was old; it seemed
unwelcoming, severe: Beryl had carefully preserved

this austere "Old France" appearance, desired by old man Bohun, which inspired confidence.

Christophe watched the grey crowd of workers flow, the worn hats, rolled black umbrellas held close to the chest, old overcoats; he heard the murmur of wheezing breath again, of sighs, interrupted by the first autumn coughs rising up out of the multitude. Someone he passed had half-opened a window, but the air from the street was itself limp and heavy, charged with a vaguely nauseating odour, like that exhaled from a Metro entrance. Christophe heard: "If you get home before me, Charles, put the soup on the stove…"

– If it's raining I'll wait for you in the Metro corridor…

– A two roomed flat with four kids, I don't know whether you realise that slave-labour's preferable…

Here and there, between the overcoats and dark trilbies, the red colour of a woman's hat burst out like an obstinate cry of hope. Christophe slowed down to avoid being jostled, to avoid seeing them, or hearing them. " They smile, they go on talking when they ought to be fleeing the sight of fellow human beings and wishing them dead, or themselves!"

Finally, they disappeared.

Beneath the door of the Beryl offices, a ray of light could still be seen. The shiny little copper plate bearing the name Beryl.

The boss…

How many times, Christophe thought, had he seen Beryl, when he was still only called Biruleff, bent in front of him, in front of James Bohun's son... Beryl was a fat man with soft flesh, pale and quivering like a jelly; on seeing him, every time the same association of ideas formed in Christophe's mind; he remembered enormous, cold, white sturgeons, laid out on a plate, whose cloudy opaque eyes seemed to cast a final haughty and scornful look. His hair was red and thin, reduced to small spaced out, woolly, copper curls, no longer thick enough to be slicked down flat or used to reduce the shininess of his cranium. He spoke in an always half suppressed voice, low and whispering, as if he feared that once pronounced, each word would be repeated and denatured by mortal enemies: "Ah! Monsieur Christophe Bohun", he would murmur on seeing him, and without offering his hand, would move it feebly from afar, making a grimace of a smile.

– The old rogue, Christophe thought, but he noted with satisfaction the stir of hatred that disturbed his gloomy torpor. Just at that moment, the handle on the door turned, and Beryl came out. Christophe touched the brim of his hat; Beryl did the same with a cold glance. Then he pulled his grey bowler further down his large pale face and descended; Christophe followed more slowly, behind him.

– What's he thinking? Christophe thought ironically, with a weary curiosity, no doubt something like "started with nothing... founded an important business, universally recognised".

He remembered Beryl's speech, delivered the previous night:

– The great, the only idea in my life, the prosperity of France…

And why not? This man who had begun life in the pay of James Bohun, Christophe's father, this obscure little agent who had touted some orders for Bohun, traded in steel and oil for him, now rich, married, stabilised like laundered money, was thirsty, like everybody, for consideration, respect and love. Why not? "Messieurs, I have devoted my life to an idea, to the promotion of French influence abroad, by peaceful means."

Christophe repeated it to himself in an undertone, smiling; he looked at the view of the huge round back, already disappearing in the gloom of the lower floors. What else did he say?

– We others, Latins…

– This little Jew, born on the borders of Romania, my father's most trusted agent…Despite everything, it's funny…

On the threshold he abruptly mused:

– And no doubt it was only when he saw me that he had the idea: started from nothing! And now the son, the real son of the ruined James Bohun, works in my business, mixed in with the anonymous mass of my employees!... He shrugged his shoulders, pushed the bolts with a tired, bitter little grimace, murmured smiling:

– To hell with it!...and left.

It was an October evening, part rain, part light. Now and again the wind blew in gusts, carrying a strong pure scent redolent of the country and open plains. Beyond the black clouds the horizon was yellow; the pavement wet, slippery and shining. Among the crowd some tanned, golden-necked boys, brought to mind past holidays and the sea.

A woman was looking at Christophe. He was past forty, a large, lean, youthful body, hard face, older than his age, bony nose, small disdainful mouth, deeply arched at the corners; on his upper lip a short tobacco-stained moustache was strewn with white hairs.

– Perhaps? the woman could be seen thinking, why not?

She stared at him, smiled; he had lowered his piercing eyes, and the large bulging eyelids, veiled with long eyelashes, leant a nonchalant, dreamy expression to his whole face.

The woman slowed her pace and, after a moment, stopped. But he fled the street without looking at her, where, in the darkening sky, some neon lights, spasmodically went off and on, forming a flaming crown

B..E..R..Y..L..

at the top of the building and lower down:

B..　E..　R..　Y..　L..　　　N..　E..W..　S A..G..E..N..C..Y..

2

The cars were moving forward slowly toward the Opéra, flowing like a black river, criss-crossed with fiery reflections, coming to a halt every minute or so, stuck in a jam. They gave off an unearthly clamour, sharp rings, the sound of hooters, the groaning of wheels on the greasy autumn ground. Nobody turned a hair. Passers-by carried along in parallel streams, continued to jostle each other without noticing. They clenched their fists on the handles of their open umbrellas, bent their backs, hurried, their tired eyes seemed to be looking inward, as if each one of them contemplated, in the depths of their soul, his own familiar little serpent, daily worry.

Christophe climbed into his stationary car, folded the papers he had just bought and threw them to the floor, took the wheel, looked irritably at the motionless police officer and the horse shimmering with rain, waited impatiently for the whistle to set them moving, exhaled a little sigh, swore in an undertone, disappeared.

As always, he stopped in a neighbouring road, in front of a small bar, still dark and empty. The barman was dozing behind the counter. When he saw Christophe come in, he got up, shook the shaker mechanically, switched on the light bulbs, and waited for an order.

Christophe sat down; he leant his long body across the counter till he could feel the iron rail pressing against his chest. He sighed deeply, said, as on every night:

– Quarter of champagne, José.

Little by little the light trembling that agitated his hands ceased. He asked:

– OK?

Without hearing the reply, he took his paper, held it in front of him, crumpled it distractedly, threw it down, unfolded another one. He wasn't reading. He was just scanning the headlines with a gloomy eye. "Fall of the dollar... Unemployment... crisis... budget deficit... Hunger march on London... Unemployment... crisis..."

He swallowed the first glass down without leaving his lips time to taste the flavour. At this hour of the day, having not drunk alcohol since lunch, he had a searing desire, the hunger of a smoker deprived of cigarettes. He ordered a second glass, and a brandy, and mixed them himself. Little by little, the bar was filling with silent shadows. Nearly all men, leaving their petty jobs, office, bank...and coming here neither to find women, nor to cut a deal, but simply to drink, and to be quiet, to replenish their energy for the hard task that remained ahead, before the all-pitying night: the family dinner.

For eight years, Christophe had met them every evening at the same time. He scarcely knew their names. They never exchanged a word other than a brief:

– OK?...

and a nod of the head...

He played a silent game of dice or shared drinks with one of them. But he didn't even look at him, he could scarcely distinguish his features from the others. However this particular evening, he looked up and contemplated the man beside him, like himself on a high bar-stool; and a sensation of nausea took hold. The kind one feels when one perceives one's aging image in a wardrobe mirror in the morning, in the shadow of an early dawn.

Like Christophe, this man inclined his face with a weary, troubled expression; like him, he felt around distractedly with nervous, trembling hands for the dice, scattered between two empty glasses. He was forty-five or fifty, large ears sticking out of his head, thin hair forming a pink tonsure in the middle of his skull, he had the swollen eyelids of those who spend all day writing in an office, where sunlight never penetrates, only the rays from an angle-poise with a green shade. He had large blue pockets under his eyes. He was grey, fat and weary; he smoked incessantly; panted softly, like an old dog with heart trouble.

Christophe looked mechanically at his own reflection in the mirror, uneasily touched his fingers, the hollow cheeks, the edges of his nostrils that alcohol abuse had strewn with the first blotchy little red spots, the balding temples, the crumpled corners of his eyelids.

– I'm not like him yet, but, patience, it'll happen. That's how I'll be on Sunday, he thought, with a little ironic sigh.

When they'd played two rounds and consumed the drinks that went with each win, the man raised his head, contemplated the clock showing quarter-past-seven with a gloomy stupor, sighed deeply, and closed his eyes for a second, as sick animals do, when one comes to lead them by the neck out of a dark corner where they've been lying.

He put on his overcoat, silently shook Christophe's hand and left.

Christophe checked the time as well, but he wavered, ordered another glass, the last…

To go back… To find the family all together… Geneviève, her forehead raised, waiting for the conjugal kiss, that soft-skinned forehead that creased under his lips, Philippe… Murielle… Memories of the past, sick old Bohun, the dinner, dark and silent, life…

– Life…

He clenched his teeth. Often when he was most exasperated with this evening ritual (for no valid reason) a savage little grimace twisted his lips.

The barman, recognising the sign that an order was going to follow, took his glass asking:

– Same again, monsieur?

Christophe lowered his head, made an effort of memory, asked:

– How's your wife, old man?

José's wife suffered from tuberculosis, coughed out her lungs in a sanatorium of the Ville de Paris, situated between the black fir trees of Vosges. He was a twenty-year-old little Spaniard, with a thin girlish face, yellow as an orange.

He raised his head:

– Always the same.

He pushed the plate of olives towards him, hesitated, lowered his eyes as a livid redness covered his face, and said:

– It's sad, isn't it, because she's isn't old?

The barman seemed to calculate, spread out his hands:

– Twenty. Just like me...it's hard luck...

– Dirty old life, said Christophe.

– Dirty old life, monsieur, said the barman.

One by one, the clients left. The engine-hum of little Citroëns and Renaults outside the door could be heard. The boss came by and put out the lights at the back. Bohun remained alone. Eight o'clock... Just this last glass, abruptly resigned to leaving, he swallowed it in one, almost immediately stopped himself, feeling tipsy. He was so habituated to alcohol that usually it took more than five glasses to feel drunk. But today, he was tireder than usual. The champagne absorbed over the course of an hour, to which this extra throat full was added, went briskly to his head, set his blood alight. He pressed his cheek to his hand, closed his eyes. How much better, how much more acerbic, more violent than love... His head turned, spun, his heart throbbed in rapid beats; fire ran in his veins. For no reason he felt like laughing. He looked at the little Spaniard, smiling.

– *Never mind, old fellow!... Cheer up!...*, he said in English.

The Spaniard murmured sadly, without understanding:

– Of course, monsieur.

Christophe got off his barstool heavily, paid, went out. He started up the car and drove toward the embankments. He lived in avenue Marceau. Suddenly he noticed that he'd taken a wrong road and was crossing the Seine.

– I'm drunk, he murmured.

But the rain which was falling in bursts and lashing his face through the lowered windows, sobered him up quickly. He glanced at the Seine, at the yellow sky and tumultuous autumn, then, slowly, turned around.

In one second, the low spirits, chased away by alcohol vapours, had once again invaded. He huffed with anger, but looked fondly at the black car-bonnet on which the rain was beating, rebounding off in diamond sparks, thinking:

– The only pleasure on earth…

And he returned to the avenue Marceau.

3

The Bohuns lived at the end of avenue Marceau, a tall corner house looking out over the Seine; old James Bohun had installed himself there during a period of splendour, at the time of Christophe's birth; the apartment had remained the same, vast and sombre. It still contained some huge pieces of furniture, a few dark indecipherable paintings, the gilt from a frame shining here and there in the shadows. The rest had been auctioned off in 1925, at the time of the Bohun crash.

Christophe went in.

Geneviève came to meet him, offered her forehead, said:

– Good evening my darling…

and:

– It's probably time to get out your winter coat?...

– Not yet, my darling, he replied, before they passed each other in the dining room.

It was hung with a dark green ribbed material which became black under the lights. Of the four verdure tapestries of Flanders, only one remained, whose authenticity was doubtful; the room was lit by an electric bulb, bright and crude, which brutally illuminated people's faces.

There were four of them round the table. Christophe, his wife, their son Philippe aged eighteen, and Murielle de Pena, a niece of old Bohun.

The old man took his meals in his bedroom, which he hadn't left for a long time. Little by little, he had abandoned the rest of the apartment to his children; he only kept two rooms for himself, where he remained alone, nearly all day, sitting in the same armchair, in the corner by the fire. He suffered from a malady of indeterminate origin, consisting of prolonged fever, cough, spitting blood and general inflammation, his thinness got worse from day to day.

Once, when Philippe came up to him, old James, smiling weakly in his feeble breathless voice, had said to a pale-faced Geneviève;

– It's life that's burnt up my lungs, my girl, not the disease that you fear.

Besides, it was rare for Philippe to enter his grandfather's room, and when he did appear, the old man usually contented himself with putting his hand in his pocket and asking with his slow smile:

– How much?

– Poor man, Geneviève said.

But she didn't finish; she never allowed herself any signs of disapproval other than a raising of the head, a pale resigned smile, and, sometimes, a little movement of pursed lips and a sigh: "He's embittered, poor man, you have to feel sorry for him…"

In the depths of his soul (as she was so good, so benevolent, so musical, so proficient at sewing, knitting, embroidering, mending, making perfect cakes and stews, and knowing "how to hold her own in the world", and how to make love) Christophe called her "Madame de Fleurville", the perfect mother of model little girls. However, nineteen years earlier in 1915, when she was looking after him in the old provincial house, under a roof holed with shells, he had loved her, he had even ardently desired her... how fresh and tranquil she had seemed, with her long golden hair, her beautiful calm face, her limpid modulated voice... And how quickly he'd wearied of her... But he hadn't yet arrived at that blissful stage of conjugal life, where one ceases even to notice one's spouse, whose forgotten face is mixed up with the furniture and the mute bedrooms. He continued to be conscious of her presence, to nurse a suppressed anger toward her; her words, her supposed thoughts, her movements, her little habits, irritated him all the time, her absence was agreeable, but when he thought that one day she might die before him, he felt penetrated by a sharp pain.

She was talking to Murielle, who, as usual, replied distractedly while tapping the tablecloth with the ends of her fingers.

– But how so...of course...but certainly my darling...

without even pretending to listen.

She said:

– My poor friend, that's the way the world is. We can't change it, neither you nor I. Beryl's wife is an unfortunate woman, I pity her. When a young girl's badly brought up and badly supervised, it's not surprising that once married she conducts herself... let's say the word, since it's not a young girl here but a shameless woman. The poor soul, she's preparing a sad old age for herself. Ah! if Philippe had been a girl...

– What happiness, Christophe thought with a little retrospective shiver, that at least would've saved me…

She became silent sighing. Her face once again agreeable in repose, features slightly swollen, the lower part puffy and the flesh, florid.

But Christophe sometimes took a kind of pleasure in watching her; she never changed; she withered, but without anything having been transformed, without doing away with anything, like a maturing fruit, increasing in size, but keeping its original appearance… Not like Murielle, ravishing in the past, light and vivacious, the dark crown of her hair hanging in tresses curling around her face, her large sparkling green eyes, her long angled eyebrows; who had become this sullen ageing woman, always wrapped in a shawl or a woollen cardigan that she didn't do up, that she left hanging from her shoulders, pulling it from minute to minute in a vague and weary way. Her marriage, her divorce, hard times, and worries had extinguished her, as a flame goes out behind a window covered in ice and snow.

Geneviève turned toward her husband.

– And you, darling, you're not saying anything. Nothing new at the office?

– Of course not, Christophe said, shrugging his shoulders imperceptibly. But she continued to look questioningly. He muttered with an impatient expression:

– What do you want there to be?

– No difficulties?

– Of course not... everything's alright... it's always the same...

What new could happen in the office? I mean good things, and for the rest, we're spoilt for choice. (In a neighbouring bank, twenty-five employees dismissed again the previous night...) "One of the blessed of the world, Christophe mused with a bitter little grimace, three thousand francs a month, a well-paid job, certainly for what I do..."

He came back to himself thinking of the mechanical nature of his job, the daily routine, the empty hours spent in an overheated office where the Remingtons clicked incessantly in the half-silence, like the nibbling of mice in the wainscoting of an old house, which one ends up not hearing. And towards evening, these two hours, two and a half hours of stupid work, letters to be directed to one service or another...For eight years, it hadn't changed, in truth it would never change.

Beryl feared him, the son of his old boss, the steel Bohun, the Bohun of the good old days; the redoubtable reputation of his name was such that people trembled to see him approach too close to the workings of the business, that whenever possible, they avoided involving him in anything relating to management, to its schemes, to all the mysteries in which they were enveloped...

– If they could only know, Christophe thought lazily, how much I couldn't give a damn.

He detested his useless work, but, since the crash, there had only been a monthly income of two thousand francs in the old Bohun household, together with the free living for him and his family.

One had to dress, pay for the car, holidays, everything that made life tolerable.

– It's certainly necessary, he thought to himself again, it's certainly necessary, as Geneviève said, to do as everybody does…

He forced a smile:

– Poor Geneviève…

– He's an idler, said Geneviève, of such and such of their friends, with an expression of disgust. And a man who doesn't work, isn't a man.

Besides, quite visibly, she hadn't yet lost all hope of seeing her husband's career, one day crowned with success, "success, the fruit of labour…"

– Damnation, Christophe said to himself.

– Murielle, Geneviève said, really, you must fix your black dress. How you've let yourself go… she finished, in a soft reproachful tone, which unconsciously concealed under its airy lightness, a vicious female triumph.

Murielle, with a little unconcerned smile, arranged the collar that adorned her old black dress, said in an undertone:

– It's fine like this, I assure you…Could I light a cigarette?...Dinner is finished…

– Only the compote, darling…

– We finally viewed the whole film this morning, Philippe, second assistant for six months at the Q.J.L.O. Studios, said half-heartedly.

Christophe didn't reply, but Geneviève indulgently asked:

– Was it good love?

Philippe pulled a face. He spoke extremely slowly, as if he was eating, as if he was doing all sorts of things, seeming to fear giving away his thoughts, a piece of his genius, to relatives at too low a price. He looked like his father; he was tall and thin like him, with a large nose and dilated nostrils, a heavy chin, but his eyes were those of the Courtenays, his mother's family, grey eyes, shimmering, bordered by thick black eyelashes.

– That little Laurette Lacy fucked the whole thing.

– Come on, dear, Geneviève murmured painfully, that coarse word, uttered at the family table in front of your parents!... have you lost your head?...

However, she is pretty, she added after a moment's thought.

Philippe curled his lips.

– She isn't repugnant, he conceded at last, with a little exasperated sigh. And besides, there are some good things in the film. The last scene has a great rhythm.

He uttered his words as if he was casting pearls before swine, then stopped talking.

Christophe Bohun ate silently, looking at his wife and son.

– He's so affected, that boy…

Why do they all have the *mouth* of an undiscovered Pascal at that age? Why do they dress so badly?

He said aloud, almost in spite of himself:

– Don't you think if you ordered some detachable collars one millimetre higher, everything else staying just as it suits you, your profile would be pleasanter to look at?...

– H'm... Philippe muttered softly: people wear them like this, papa, you don't know...

– If it isn't too much bother, would you be so kind as to pass me the salt.

– Eh? What? The salt? murmured Philippe, as if waking from a dream: oh, yes...

– Good God, thought Christophe.

He hated Philippe's narrow jackets just as much as his low collars, from which a long thin adolescent neck emerged, reddish, with prominent Adam's apple; his affected posture of unruffled calm "aloofness", his "greats", his "not repugnants", when he said that a girl was pretty, his "I'm madly in loves", often uttered, while maintaining the iciest of looks, fixed and distracted, seeming to perceive his parents with difficulty, in the distance, like smoke, or vague shadows. This disconcerting Philippe... Christophe was well aware however that he knew nothing about him, like all fathers everywhere, only the most misleading superficial appearances. Between Philippe and himself, the memory of Philippe as a child, born when Christophe himself was still young... the child that he'd loved... was superimposed like a mask placed over a face. He remembered one of James Bohun's words and his smile: "Come on, don't shower too much love on your son, Kit, you'll expect him to give it back to you later. Bad deal."

Perhaps...Philippe, at the age of four, or eight...his cries, his laugh..."Papa!..." He closed his eyes, listened desperately to that infant voice from the depths of the past, bright and fresh, which had broken, which wasn't yet a man's voice, but rather had a false high-pitched timbre that pained his musical ear... Little Philippe... His golden curls, coated now with a thick layer of Brylcreem, a sort of oily carapace, putting off Geneviève's maternal hand.

Finishing a discussion that he hadn't heard the beginning of, but which repeated itself night after night, Geneviève was saying:

– In spite of everything, my love, I'm sorry you didn't pursue your studies. We live in a topsy-turvy world, but intellectual culture, and degrees...

– Oh! papa has them... for all the good it does him, murmured Philippe with a light inflexion of pity.

– I fully understand, Christophe said, but...

And, abruptly, comforting himself, he displaced his son's attack onto his own father: ... but at least, I won't have the Bohun crash to offer you as a joyful gift of inheritance.

He became silent, shrugged his shoulders, it was rare for him to allow himself words which he considered pointless. And when it happened, he observed himself from a distance with sarcasm, as if someone else had said them, and noted the offence.

– Stupid, grotesque... scarcely twenty-five years older than this little one and talking like an old man...

Twenty-five years!...he suddenly thought, feeling overwhelmed.

Philippe's words and their scornful tone had moved a deep, hidden, store of bile in his soul. It was certainly true that old man Bohun had never helped him...In the past he gave money without taking account...but his business affairs had always been a closed book...

– Besides, they never interested me, Christophe thought, what am I complaining about?

He looked with aversion at the fruit bowl presented by the servant for a second time:

– These dinners... too healthy, too light, they can't even dull the mind, or take the edge off one's worries...

Will you serve the cognac in the living room with the coffee, Juliette...

– Christophe, murmured Geneviève, your liver... I beg you, do it for me, stop drinking...no brandy, Juliette; OK my darling? Are you coming, Murielle? What are you dreaming about, my darling?... You're always somewhere on the moon, she finished, in a gentle tone of reproach.

They got up and moved into the little living room.

Geneviève said:

– I saw your typist, Mlle Belcolor... she had a very elegant hat! Really, for an employee... But these girls...

The scornful curve of the lips when she spoke of a woman susceptible to being looked at by her husband, was the only thing that animated the ordinarily unmoving, too fleshy, too blooming face, in a cruel, human expression, Christophe thought ...

It happened when she watched Murielle, believing herself unobserved… she gently brought her eyelashes together, so that only a gleaming flash of light could filter between her half-closed eyelids, like a knife… "Poor Geneviève …"

– …Naturally, these girls only think of being noticed by their boss…

On the threshold, Murielle yawned softly:

– I'm sleepy, I'm going to lie down, she said.

She ran her hands through her hair, rummaging slowly in the loose locks. The red on her lips had worn off, she redid it with her finger, caught Christophe's glance, shrugged her shoulders, turned around with a slight frown. She looked at him for a second, challengingly. He read her thoughts: "And for whom to be beautiful now? For whom to make-up, dress-up, live?" Christophe, involuntarily felt a cruel, ironic pleasure, like some obscure kind of vengeance. "Why, he thought immediately, surprising himself: Why? Is it because she's changed? and I see time passing more in her?..."

He was ashamed of his feelings, took her hand and kissed it.

She went out of the room.

How tired Murielle seems, said Geneviève.

She was thinking to herself:

– He took her hand with such tenderness… No, no, one shouldn't think, above all, one shouldn't remember, she said to herself abruptly, with a superstitious dread: "Everything's fine, the world's fine, and even if it isn't, what's the use of recriminations? One has to be resigned, close one's eyes, don't think, above all, don't think…"

4

They crossed the cold dark drawing-room without stopping; coffee was served in the old smoking room, where some wrecks from the past still survived: a chaise longue, a bridge table and two Chippendale armchairs.

Christophe and Philippe each drank several cups; they had a shared pension for strong black coffee that old Bohun had handed down, who'd only ever liked things that were harsh, bitter and strong.

Geneviève lit a small table lamp and began to knit hurriedly, reading a book held between her knees at the same time, as if she was scared of wasting precious, irreplaceable minutes. She stopped herself from time to time and let slip:

– Enough…enough coffee, Philippe and you too, Christophe, you're going to make yourself ill, I assure you… what strange tastes…

She said again:

– Your father wasn't so well this evening, Christophe, …

All of a sudden, Christophe threw himself in an armchair, eyes closed, face sunken and old looking.

He took a cigarette, rolled it several times between his fingers, inhaled some puffs at regular intervals, threw it in the fire, got up and began to pace the room with slow heavy steps. This irritated his wife and son, just as he'd been irritated by the little sighs which rose mechanically from her chest and Philippe's nonchalant affected pose, buried in the corner of an armchair…

It was a peaceable family evening…

Finally, he stopped in front of the fire, and ground his teeth in a habitual nervous tic, he presented each of his soles alternately to the flames. These vast rooms were cold, one lit the fire early in the season, when outside the mild autumn days ended in a night of soft humid sweetness.

One more time, since she'd come to live with her father-in-law, Geneviève murmured, shivering:

– I'd have preferred a small, four-roomed modern apartment, with central heating...

She didn't finish and gave a hostile look at the heating vents, which only granted their parsimonious whiffs of unhealthy heat from November to March. Nobody replied. Philippe, since he was thinking that when his parents, enriched by the expected inheritance from old James Bohun (of which nobody spoke, but everybody hoped), lived in the apartment of their dreams; he would be a Hollywood film director (the magic words filled his soul with a kind of drunken pain: Hollywood, Santa Monica, Beverley Hills, that didn't come easily...In the end, there was no point in complaining...Bitch of a life, even so... They're happy with it, the old folk...)

He sighed ironically. Christophe loved this old lounge, vast and devastated, just as he loved everything dark and silent, with a deep, melancholic pleasure.

However, Philippe, in his corner, was absent-mindedly turning the knobs on the wireless. Some vibrations filled the room, then faded, changed into a bizarre whistling, went off, came back more highly pitched, only to cease abruptly.

What seemed like a waltz, some far off violin chords, some rapid speech in an incomprehensible language, that sometimes increased in volume like thunder, and sometimes whispered from the depths of space, cut across by the slow, throaty voice of the French announcer:

"...On the Brittany coast, wind and rain, low temperatures."

Christophe impatiently murmured:

– Leave that for the love of God...

Philippe, without hearing him, continued to twist and untwist the knobs, content to voice an inarticulate mutter from time to time:

"H'm... Yes... Wait... right now..."

A man's voice announced itself so distinctly that it made Christophe jump:

– One can already see signs that the new generations are reacting against the excessive importance accorded to material things... Above all, young people appreciate spiritual values...A new way of being will soon be apparent, a romantic conception of love... Love will once again become a reality...It will consecrate itself to the joys of love...

– Did you hear that, Christophe said softly.

Philippe looked up, regarded him with a sort of astonishment and irony, as if he was dreaming:

– Really, they think that?...

And Christophe returned his gaze.

– Long live love, said the orator.

Geneviève sighed.

Philippe changed wavelengths. The talk ended.

A soft, muffled strum of guitars and a far off female voice, light and passionate, crossed the sad dark room like a swarm of bees, and lost itself in the shadows.

– A Spanish music concert, said Geneviève.

Christophe had closed his eyes for a moment with an expression of silent pleasure, but Philippe had already turned the knob, and, immediately some indecipherable words, the marketplace, shouts: "…crisis, fall, unemployment, Ohio farmers protest against Roosevelt's policies, the House votes for new taxes", all these different cries, joined together, melted into the same hateful gloomy clamour, seemed to penetrate the secluded room from outside.

Exasperated, Christophe got up and walked out, slamming the door violently.

Geneviève yawned softly, spread out the knitting on her knees.

– Twelve more rows, she murmured, rapidly counting the stitches from the end of the long steel needle: shut the door my love. Your father just closed it but it's opened again after him. I can feel a cold draught from the dining room, she added shuddering lightly.

In a lower voice, she repeated, one more time, sighing:

– I never liked this house.

5

Christophe had gone into his father's bedroom; a coke fire glowed feebly in the chimney place; in the shadows, in the depths of a large armchair, old James Bohun was ensconced.

He was an elderly man with a delicate, fragile appearance, pale skin seemingly devoid of any blood, silver hair, deeply ringed hollow eyes, which must once have been beautiful, and which despite the lassitude of fever and age, still retained a diamond-like sparkle, a limpid black colour.

He was watching the fire, his hands clasped on his knees, immobile, a newspaper fallen at his feet. He seemed to be half asleep.

When his son entered, he said in a low voice, which he deliberately lowered even more, in order to spare his worn out vocal cords.

– Yes. Come in.

– How are you, papa?

He didn't reply, shrugged his shoulders gently, then asked:

– How's the weather today?

– Bad. Rain and wind.

Seated opposite his father, Christophe silently watched "the steel Bohun" poking the fire and coughing, the one of whom they used to say: "…in his footsteps ruin and war…" He had never known him other than with long silver hair, a sad abused expression, that penetrating ironic smile. He didn't speak much; his few gestures, his looks, his silences signified clearly: "Leave me alone. Don't meddle in my affairs as I don't meddle in yours. I don't need you. Neither your help, nor your love, nor your safe-keeping. I don't give anything, but I ask for nothing in return. Leave me in peace."

Every now and again, a deep hacking cough shook his chest and shoulders. He lifted his hand gently to reclaim the silence and seemed to listen with detachment to the cough, which resonated in the depths of his lungs. He took a long breath and dilated his nostrils with an effort. A deep crackle rose from his chest and then subsided. He began to speak again in a low soft voice:

– What's new?

– Nothing, father.

– Business?

– Bad, father.

– Yours?...

– Beryl's?...

He indicated yes, already exhausted with having spoken, his lips half-open and trembling.

Christophe said:

– Always the same thing, at least what I'm involved with...

– Nobody's been laid off?

– No, said Christophe, not for the moment...

– They'll keep you, don't worry, said Bohun. Even after I'm dead... I've sorted it... At least you don't have to worry about that, he murmured after a moment's reflection, with a tired little grimace – the only physical trait that Christophe had got from him. He had become slightly animated while speaking. His cheeks, whose transparent pallor was astonishing, became feverishly dark red.

Christophe thought involuntarily:

– If that assurance is all he's counting on leaving me…

And once again, the same obsessive preoccupation began in his mind, as if set in motion by a delicate mechanism:

– They say that he put aside eight or ten million after the crash… If it was only five, or four million… That money, where did it come from?... How did he manage to save it from his creditors?... Ah! I don't know anything about it, too bad, it's his business… If, from his fabulous past fortune, he could leave his son just enough to live and be sure of tomorrow… It's true that security's a currency that's no longer tendered. Lord, to be delivered from money… from money worries!... from what they call bread-winning!...

He closed his eyes, repeating mentally, like a prayer:

– To be delivered from money!...

The steel Bohun, the oil Bohun, everything he sold, everything he bought… He looked at his father's hands, those pale hands, which seemed bloodless, which tried twice to pick up the heavy poker…

– It's a pity that I'm not close enough to ask him to tell me his life-story. He'll die soon, and I'll know nothing. I'll never know anything.

Even the crash, he only knew what the papers at the time had reported. A mass of tittle-tattle, rumours, nothing. He suddenly remembered this journalist, who came to interview his father during that period. Bohun wouldn't let him in; he contented himself with getting Christophe to pass him a card with these words: "James Bohun has lost his voice, and can no longer sing." Christophe smiled. " Yes, his life must have been … strange…"

– Is it true, Bohun asked, that Rollers and Vicks have merged?...

– I don't know, Christophe said with indifference.

– What do you do all day at the office, son? asked old man Bohun. And his deep scoffing way of uttering the word "son", as if he was valuing the true worth of a son, his flesh and blood, a burdensome branch cut off, a useless luxury, caused a frisson of anger to pass through Christophe's heart.

– I wait for the evening, he said.

Bohun murmured with a slight smile:

– The new generation has elevated laziness to the level of a religion.

Christophe asked abruptly:

– Father?... You always loved it?...

– What? said James raising his eyebrows slightly.

Christophe hesitated:

– That life…

– Yes, I loved that life, the old Bohun murmured in his flat passionless voice. But his eyes were sparkling, alight with a fire flaming with fever and regret. He looked at his son with an expression of unspeakable scorn, said softly:

– You wouldn't understand my boy…

He stopped himself, made a tired movement, shivered.

– The cold's beginning… You'd better put the draught-excluders on the doors, Kit…

– Have you got money? Kit asked suddenly, thinking of the end of the coming month, as his father frequently covered expenses that he'd forgotten to settle.

The old Bohun winced again; blood rose into his pale transparent cheeks like a river of fire.

– He's getting old, Christophe thought, with conscious and painful cruelty: before, nobody would have been able to read the thoughts on his face like this…

But that voice, that breathless whispering, which moved him, in spite of himself, to the bottom of his heart, no less soft or modulated, replied:

– I'll give you the money…

He began to cough again. But this time the coughing fit didn't stop. It gradually became more violent sending him, bent double, head in arms, toward the little table, pushed in front of the fire. He tried to get his breath back, and immediately the cough resounded and wheezed in his chest, like the sound of wind in an empty chimney.

– What can I do? asked Christophe.

James Bohun made an effort to hold his breath for a moment; his eyes were injected with blood. He cried brusquely, with a kind of hatred.

– Nothing!... Nothing!... You can't do anything!...

He finished in a softer voice:

– Naturally…

And almost immediately, the coughing fit started up, bending him over again.

Christophe, resigned, looked at the time. Every evening at the same time the coughing crisis took hold of old Bohun. One heard it in the neighbouring rooms until morning, this terrible raucous cough that made the servants shudder.

– My God, how does he stay alive? He hasn't got any lungs…

But he wasn't dying.

A half hour went by. He refused to take the medicine that Christophe offered. Finally, the cough settled, he took the tranquillising tablet, brought it to his lips, mastered the trembling of his hands with an effort, and swallowed it. And immediately he put his handkerchief to his mouth, and withdrew it, stained with fresh blood.

– There you are, he whispered.

He looked at Christophe without saying anything. But Christophe read the thoughts in his eyes: " You pity yourself. Sort yourself out. You're young. Look, I'm coughing my lungs out. Look. I'm dying. You? What do you and yours mean to me?... Lies, one doesn't love one's children more than oneself!...One loves… at least oneself, I only loved myself, only my life, only me!..."

And Christophe thought:

– If this has to finish…well it's better that it finishes as quickly as possible!...

He added inwardly:

– To bring an end to his suffering.

But, at the bottom of his heart, in the depths of his consciousness, were wishes, inchoate reveries, like dreams just before sleep: "If I had his money more quickly…" he thought.

He paled. He stood up, back to the fire, watched the overwhelmed old man, eyes closed, hands clasped to his handkerchief soaked in blood, with a strange feeling of anguish that gripped his heart. And, suddenly he felt invaded by pity, an obscure, painful tenderness.

– My poor father, he said in an undertone.

James Bohun forced a smile, rested his head back on the little, chequered green leather cushion that supported his neck, said softly:

– I'm tired. I want to sleep.

When Christophe returned to the lounge, Philippe had gone. Geneviève was knitting with great concentration, repeating mechanically out loud:

– One dropped, one stitch, one dropped, one stitch, one dropped, one, two, three, four stitches, one dropped, one stitch, and I begin again…

On seeing her husband come in, she looked at the time, and said, as she did every night with an expression of relief, as her long day was finally coming to an end, there's no other cure for life than to lose oneself in darkest sleep, deepest sleep, with as few dreams as is possible to imagine:

– Ah, it's nearly eleven o'clock. Let's go to bed.

They slept side by side, seeking by habit the warmth of their neighbouring bodies. The cold wind blew through the open window. In spite of the bedroom that separated them from the vast empty lounge, they could hear old James coughing. His son imagined him sitting in front of the fire, coughing, poking, and thinking… no longer dreaming of anything, without doubt... He was no more than a cadaver, a body without a soul.

– Ah, how I hate life, he nearly said out loud on going off to sleep, while he mentally chanted in a sort of dull, weary cantilena: " Shit, oh shit, shit, shit..."

Geneviève moved. Her arms came out of the covers, looking in the obscurity with her fingers, for the little electric lamp fixed on her bedside table, switched it on. She looked at the time, asked:

– You said something, my darling?

– No, my darling, said Christophe. Go to sleep...

They went to sleep.

6

James's housekeeper half-opened the door.

– Monsieur is going to lie down?

James shook his head without responding. To lie down, to stretch out, so that blood would immediately flow toward his throat and stifle him even more…

– I'll have plenty of time to sleep, he thought. All eternity…

The housekeeper left. The old man continued to watch the fire. He went on struggling with his laboured breathing: the smallest whiff of air that passed through his throat woke the dormant cough at the base of his chest.

– I wonder how long this can go on for… he thought once again. I wonder…

Nobody knew whether the illness had provoked or delayed that incomprehensible, that famous Bohun crash…In order to live the life he had been living, you needed a will taut as a bow, nervous energy that only health and youth could sustain…This low-grade fever every evening at the same time, this slight shiver between the shoulders, the tiredness, the blood on the lips, this exhausting cough, these pains in the back, in the hollow of the kidneys, all that had destroyed him, had beaten him… That, and not men…

– Ah! if I was young and strong again. It's not true that times have changed… The crisis, the lack of money, what nonsense… They don't know, the men of today, that's all… I…But this mortal indifference…what's the good, dear God, a question of six months or one more year?...One can't buy a new heart and lungs...And anyway...I've tasted everything, known everything, he thought again, with a sort of bitter pride. It's for others, for others now...I give up my turn willingly...I'm tired.

The fire was going out. He contemplated the pile of coals and glowing cinders with half-closed eyes for some time; the old wood crackling softly in the shadows.

He stretched out his hand, mechanically touched the small table, got the box of cough-pills ready to take...to suppress his cough...to contain this intolerable suffering, this sensation of an open wound in his chest. He brought his hand to his throat carefully.

– My father died this way, he thought, and my brother...

He remembered the little money-changing kiosk in the Greek port where he was born, the narrow street bordered by tavernas and sailors' brothels. His father's house, with its shaky wooden terrace, the floors, from which a cloud of dust rose up when a foot was applied with any pressure... in the courtyard, a dried up poplar that the autumn wind shook with such strange and deep groans... He leaned his head slightly to one side, making an effort to hear his father's cough, which penetrated the house every night... A distant image formed in his memory... Himself, as a child, and his brothers, sleeping in the little lower bedroom, the candle lit in the window, the flame agitated by the sea-breeze, a white sail, which moved slowly in the distance, lit by the full moon, filled out in the shadows, like a delicate blooming flower…the tiled floor, the muffled cries from the house opposite, where the whores and sailors drank…And the noise, above his head, of footsteps and his father's cough, mixed with the jingling of moving coins.

His mother… A Levantine, face covered in white powder infiltrated by grease, but in the folds of flesh, two eyes sparkled, the same as his own…Christophe had inherited nothing from her, nor from him…Christophe had his own mother's face. He was blond like her. As a child he had her delightful face. Now…What a strange being…"If he'd listened to me, old James thought, but he always begged to differ, an empty life…" What exactly did he want…Lord!… To be young like him, healthy like him, with a heart, good solid lungs, blood boiling in the veins, and not to know, not even to want to become the richest and most powerful of men…Deceptive power, without doubt, but intoxicating… He thought of his brother, of Murielle's father…if he had lived…that youthful energy, that fever, but he died, without leaving a son. Only this alien, Christophe, remained, who wasn't interested in anything he liked, neither business, nor gambling, nor women. Little Philippe was nothing but a bourgeois, a Courtenay…

James Bohun leant forward, in a more lively way. That marriage, in his heart of hearts he'd never really forgiven him. He wouldn't have dreamt of forbidding it. Good God, Christophe was old enough. But to become infatuated with that petite bourgoise, with that placid creature who couldn't have had blood hotter than a fish running through her veins. Faithful?... Devoted?... Certainly... But what did a woman's faithfulness matter?... And their tenderness only served to irritate and weaken a man. He thought of Christophe's mother, who had left him, and who had died long ago. She...He sighed:

– I really loved her, but there's no shame in that...She was beautiful, she had a lovely face, an admirable body...

In the past, before the war, when she appeared with him in one of the salons of London or Paris, where people watched him from a distance, as if he were a mysterious malevolent king... (Lord, in their imaginations they could nearly see the traces of blood on his hands, as a result of a lot of old rumours, when steel prices rose, the night before the Boer War... A load of gossips...of stories... But he had always loved to be surrounded by this aura... Moreover, God have mercy, he had always known that down here, it wasn't through pity or love that one achieved one's ends ...But he alone knew to what point one could be driven by human business, by life itself...But it was better that people believed in these legends: the masters of the world... it was better...) That woman... Yes, when he entered with that woman on his arm, everybody turned and murmured: "What a beauty..." And of old Spanish blood, so proud, that he'd bought a prize worth millions...

– But perhaps they're right?...Perhaps our time has passed...

Nowadays, he no longer read the papers, due to all the rotten scandals, trials, ruins without grandeur, into which, little by little, high international finance had sunk…only the small fry remained now, and even they were threatened by a wave of destitution that had hit the world, a tide of mediocrity and poverty… He was already so far away, so detached from everything, so old, that he no longer even had personal enemies: he could watch everything that happened with pity. Besides, he had always believed that the world was big enough for everybody…big enough for him, certainly… Coal, corn, oil, steel… Steel, above all, which had brought him an immense fortune, and which had ruined him… Yes, in 1925… steel stocks bought in the expectation of a possible war… The little Beryl agency, the name of the straw man, that he'd founded during the war, " to enhance profits from French political and economic action abroad" this "Beryl News Agency", that he'd created and which had to become strong and powerful, and hostile, naturally, it had done its best to create a state of unease and tension, in which wars broke out like natural fires in a baking summer forest… The Middle-East, England, France… Yes, everything was well sorted… Only, in 1925, nobody wanted war. Everything was going so well… There was money for everybody. One only had to put out one's hand. The whole world was fat, happy, unperturbed. Nobody dreamt that it wouldn't last, that only wars prevented this glut of gold, and that when they were stopped, one simply replaced violent death by a more gradual kind of asphyxia…But he had miscalculated, in spite of everything… He got it wrong by several years… He was obstinate too… Because basically, if his steel was used to build cannons or mowers, what difference to him? But what was really terrible in all that, was that once engaged on a certain path, you had to go step by step to the end, with your eyes open … War hadn't broken out; the price of raw materials had plummeted… At the end of 1925, the Bohun businesses showed a deficit of 400 million.

He frowned lightly at this memory. He remembered the last general meeting, the insults from those to whom, naturally, he owed the most; the fear of his accomplices, since Beryl included in its business adventures the usual suspects…He, who for months had only spoken with extreme difficulty, but he hadn't wasted his forces nor his voice in responding to them. He remembered the grey room, the evening sunset in the windows, the blood mounting to his throat, while he listened silently to the furious voices: "Traitor!... Thief!... Criminal!... Trafficker in human flesh!...

So they cried over the swallowing up of their dear money…Words, useless squawks… All the world, everybody there at least, knew that business-men didn't create ruin or war (that would really be too commodious)…but that they simply followed the crowd where it took them. The proof…one time he had really tried to unleash a war between France and England, when public opinion, when the winds were against it, it didn't happen… He let them shout. But he was, himself, a foreigner, a man without attachments, an *heimatlos,* he let himself shout out… He hadn't been naturalised like Beryl… He didn't think of politics like Beryl, this Robot…He didn't say: "We other Latins…" He smiled.

The old green long case clock, ornamented with small tortoiseshell and copper flowers ticked softly in the silence. He tidied the objects on the table mechanically, the glasses case, the small bottle of sleeping pills, the cards, the keys in their metal box. He took these keys, turned them over and over in his hand, seemed to reflect, then he got out of his armchair with difficulty, took several steps around the room, holding on to the walls. He stopped from time to time, short of breath, but each time he succeeded in suppressing the coughing crisis…As they were the worst. Normally he didn't suffer too much. Only when the cough unleashed itself, it seemed to open up a wound in his chest. At last he arrived at the desk, let himself fall into a chair, opened the drawers, one by one.

In 1925, his personal debts amounted to forty million which simply increased the deficit created by his businesses. For himself, he would never have stooped to ask a sou from anyone. But there was Christophe, and Christophe's family. And this good Beryl, compromised in the affair, had had to do what his old boss told him…They had no guts, these men. For an instant he was moved, silently, by obscure memories, then his face darkened, he lifted his head. To end up, like an old music teacher, he, James Bohun!…For the monthly payment that this trembling scoundrel made, for the job given like an almoner to his son, which ensured that Christophe wouldn't starve to death when he, Bohun, was dead. The old man willingly admitted to himself that in placing Christophe in Beryl's business, he had counted on another thing... Ah! if he'd been able to be in Christophe's shoes...But there was nothing to be done. His son bore no resemblance to him, decidedly not.

One more time, he touched the documents enclosed in a sealed envelope, with his trembling hand. The names, the dates, the exact numbers, he had marked it all, written everything down. When he was dead, Christophe would open the drawer. He was hoping for a fortune, no doubt, but wouldn't find one, on the other hand, these papers, which, in the hands of a strong young man, were worth a fortune. "If he doesn't want to understand, too bad for him...murmured old Bohun, with suppressed anger, I can't do anything else for him!..."

Once again he caught himself dreaming that he was in his son's place and that all this was falling into his own impatient hands... "Despite everything, he's my son..." But Christophe's smile and indifferent look came to mind. "I've never understood him...I'm not going to tell him all this...What's the use... I've never known how to talk", he mused again. Moreover, he's indifferent to me...It's odd...Since this stupid marriage, I haven't recognised him... An alien... He's never loved or understood what I loved... A certain taste for life, a certain strong and bitter quality to existence, he's never known it... What a generation...Weak, lazy, pitiable, cowardly...Perhaps we ate it all in advance... Perhaps their teeth are sensitive, he murmured. He repeated slowly in an undertone, with a smile: "... the parents have eaten green fruit, and the children's teeth are set on edge... Perhaps... In the end, too bad, too bad, things will sort themselves out..."

He quietly closed the drawer, got up, took the reverse route round the room, lingered for a second standing in front of the dying fire, then, with a deep sigh, let himself fall into the hollow of the armchair, began to cough again, to poke, to dream of his life passing.

7

Murielle had returned to her part of the house, and, as she did every evening, began by locking the doors. Her bedroom was the coldest, but she preferred it to all the others because she was isolated from the rest of the apartment. "What a family...", she thought to herself, "To live together, and avoid each other...Is that what's called a family, this bundle of different lives linked by necessity? However, I wouldn't want to live anywhere else...Despite the tears, the long sleepless nights in this bedroom... I love it", she thought, looking fondly at the old parquet on which she'd thrown some worn rugs, and this monumental bed, where she'd slept as a child, then as a young girl. She got undressed slowly, put on a warm dressing gown, relit the fire. She was always cold; she felt frozen to the bone. Then the long, deep, daily confrontation with the mirror began. She looked at her face. "Yes, maybe, if I hadn't got this faded look, these sad eyes and this bitter line..." She touched the light furrow which outlined delicately and deeply the sides of her nose and the corners of her mouth. " This aging face, this faded beauty... what's the point of it? Uncle James is dying. Everything's going to change, get split up... I should think about getting some money, rather than keeping my eyes fixed on a past that won't come back...How I need love, she thought, sadly. Stupid woman that I am... To love, to be loved, to feel the radiance around one, the heat of desire, of tenderness, in the end that's all I need, I only thirst for that... This is the punishment for only having loved one being in the world."

" Love, love..." She savoured the form of the word, like a fruit between her lips. " Besides, why not be frank with myself? Why say "love" and not "Christophe", since love, for me, has never had another name?... He complains, he, who's surrounded by such fervent, silent, tenderness, Geneviève's, mine?... But, without doubt, it only overwhelms him, and fills his heart with importunate pity and remorse?"

She walked around the room unthinkingly. Time went by. When she'd got undressed for the night, she looked through her books for a small blue volume of Heine... *Und was mir fehlt, du Kleine, fehlt manchem im deutschen Land...*" That's what's missing?...No! No! not that, not that, she murmured, closing the book. What good to trouble my heart more with these words, too beautiful, too sad?" She returned to her desk, took some letters, some photos, one from her husband, looked at it, reread the letter received the previous month, to which she hadn't replied:

– To try to live close to one another without demanding anything that we can't mutually offer. A presence...

To leave, and return to live with Paco?... Or go it alone, earn one's living?... They say that makes you happy. But no... Contentment, peace, perhaps a boost to one's self-esteem... But happiness, joy, only another human being who says: "I couldn't live without you..."

She lay down, shivered between the cold sheets; she forced herself to think: "Tomorrow, the hairdo and the manicure, I've scarcely got enough money till the end of the month, but, at least it'll take up two hours of my day, and with the travelling, going and coming back, if it's good weather, maybe three hours…"

8

On entering the dining room the next morning, Christophe found his wife and son sitting at the table. She was already dressed to go out, hat on head, umbrella hooked on the back of her chair. She was wearing a resigned expression, determined and serious, that Christophe recognised as being reserved for big days: clothes sales or lace and linen displays.

Opposite her, Philippe was still in pyjamas; his wild hair falling all over his face.

Christophe drank his cup of black coffee while absent-mindedly reading the paper, already scanned when getting dressed. He touched the little scab that the razor, used in haste, formed on his cheek every day, with a sense of irritation and annoyance.

Geneviève buttered the tartines, and Philippe ate them silently. Outside, the sky was grey, a fine rain was falling, rubbing delicately against the windows like the tip of a feather.

– Not going out this morning? Christophe asked at last, addressing himself to his son.

– No, he replied, sullenly. The studio's shut today, he added, lying with a sort of lazy cynicism, not that he worried about exposing part of his life to his parents, it was simply from habit since his schooldays, mechanical, like a reflex.

Christophe gave his son an almost hateful look, which focussed above all on the most obvious signs of maturity, his manliness. His chest, visible through the opening of his pyjamas, large, muscular, covered with a thick red mat, his face, still unshaven, where his moustache had grown overnight, seemed to be scattered with cinders.

Geneviève noticed the look and thinking she understood it, said reproachfully:

– Look Philippe, a bit of decency. You know how much papa disapproves of this modern couldn't care attitude, my darling…

Philippe, closed his pyjama top with a limp hand.

Christophe got up, sighing:

– Let's go.

He went out with Geneviève. As soon as he was alone, Philippe went back to bed, rolled over voluptuously under the covers, into the still warm place that his body had left between the sheets. He immersed himself in his own being, as one dives into the sea, continuing the long interrupted dream that he had been following night after night, which came from the depths of childhood, and replaced the absent fortune, uncertain love and happiness.

– Do you want a lift? Where are you going? Christophe asked in the street, looking to see the time on the red dial in the nearby pharmacy: It's annoying. I'm late.

– I'll get there just as quickly by Metro, Geneviève said. I'm going to the sales.

Christophe smiled:

– That's good. See you soon.

He left her. Geneviève disappeared under ground.

Morning and night, the Metro corridors were full of a hurrying crowd. Beneath the clock, all heads were raised simultaneously, watching the time in an anxious, irritated way, and the ants nest expanded in all directions.

Like others, Geneviève rummaged through the market with unbelievable speed, ran breathlessly between the stalls, waited impatiently for the gate to open, tapping the ground with her feet, went up into an overcrowded room, came back down with the same speed, this fever that had taken hold of her, she who was usually so calm, as soon as she'd set foot outside the apartment.

In the light autumn drizzle, a crowd of women was waiting in the street in front of the dress-shop. Drops of rain dripped off the edges of the open umbrella, down her bare neck, between the fox and the décolletage of her blouse. The women surrounding Geneviève looked just like her, they were all exactly the same, like interchangeable parts in a car-production line. They held little round umbrellas in their numbed hands, each in the same tense way, each of them angling their umbrella so as to make things as difficult as possible for their neighbour, so that the least movement would cause the umbrella ribs to get hooked under a hat. A ripple moved through the crowd, some sharp female voices muttered: "Don't push. You've trodden on my foot. I've been waiting. Wait your turn." And silence fell again. They all wore dark coats, a false fur collar, a row of artificial pearls, thin little heels that twisted cruelly on the pavement, a felt hat, and on their foreheads in an identical place, the same quiff of hair styled by the hairdresser, for the most part in the same brown colour, tinted by dye. They were made up in the same way, rouged cheeks, mouth in the shape of a cupid's bow, eyebrows looking mauve in daylight. They had an expression both of infinite patience and infinite greed, artfulness, and secret hope. They were allowed in, ten by ten, then the gate closed. They ran all over each other, elbowing, kneeing, fierce and sullen, and a smile: "Excuse me!...You can see...I was pushed..."

Those who remained behind sighed and continued their gloomy wait, with the patience of the unemployed at the doors of a soup kitchen, or cats lying in wait for a bird in the bush.

Geneviève, frowning, calculated quietly: "...Five metres, with five metres, the dressmaker could do something...but look here, what colour?...They're wearing grey, chestnut...A pretty shade of orange, perhaps... A little daring, but after all I'm not altogether an old woman..." She threw a glance in the mirror of one of the stalls, and, automatically, stood straight, with a movement common to all women, the corners of her lips lowered. She thought she wasn't ugly, not yet worn out.

– I've scarcely changed, all in all, there's the advantage of a peaceful life. While Murielle...

She raised her head:

Poor Murielle, how beautiful she used to be. But what an unhappy life, without home, without children, without purpose... I don't envy her, good God, she thought with virtuous satisfaction. Moreover, if I've stayed faithful, it's because I really wanted to. Without that, during these crazy years after the war...

She saw Bohun's house in her memory again, the sparkling chaos of the past. But she'd never liked that... And Philippe was still a child, delicate, often ill. She'd spent the prosperous times in a child's bedroom, noting down figures, sometimes on a weight-chart, sometimes on a temperature-chart.

– I don't regret anything, she thought.

Nothing... But life wasn't easy, and the future seemed dark, very uncertain... old Bohun would die soon... But when? And what would he leave?

That illness was certainly dragging on... She felt shame...

– But after all, it wasn't a question of her own father...dead long ago, moreover, he also hadn't left any other heritage than the memory of his virtues... Her father-in-law was old, poor man, and was certainly suffering!... She sighed with sincere pity: " Poor man... What a life... He was so proud, so active... He wouldn't lose much in losing his life!..."

And, yet, a shudder passed through the depths of her soul, a mixture of pity and animal fear. "To die!... Does one have to die?..." Alas, One always clings to life, without doubt even him, she thought with a sigh. However, if it's the will of God!...

– Poor man, God forbid to wish him dead!... Besides, evil to him who evil thinks, she thought with a superstitious shiver: Three million!... If only three million remained!... My God, I don't ask much in life, even so!...I've never been interested in the high life, nor luxuries... Only, a small apartment of my own, nice and tidy, where neither

Murielle's cigarettes, nor her books, nor her perfume are around… A new apartment, without memories, without a past… Only with Christophe, just the two of us until death…Maybe… maybe another child…

The doors in front of her opened.

In an instant, she brushed away these importunate thoughts, which regularly returned in the evenings and in her day-dreams. She went in. She crossed the first room, where women were yapping away, pulling at the grubby sale goods with their hands. In the neighbouring rooms, the counters were covered with half unrolled lengths of material. She went up, touched them for a long time, one by one; but they didn't appeal to her, too light, too dear, or the cuts were scarcely big enough to make a blouse. Again she thought sadly, "If I had a little girl…this would be nice for a little girl's dress…" She sighed. What a dream…But, in the early years, she hadn't wanted more children, too taken up with Philippe alone, and now, in these uncertain times, frightening… "And soon, I'll be too old", she thought melancholically.

Suddenly, her heart thrilled with pleasure. She had just seen the heavy satin crepe that she had been looking for all the time without knowing it. "She's crazy, this couturier, she thought. Greys, chestnuts!... Certainly nothing's better than black!... With my fox. A little linen collar, or lace, very simple… And yes, really, it's for now… You don't have to wish anybody dead, but it's fine to have good luck…" She insinuated herself between the women, looked at the label:

– Fifty francs. It's still pricy, but much less than in the big stores. And good quality. Let's do it, it's a good day, she thought.

9

November was approaching; it rained for weeks on end. Christophe watched the last golden leaves, weakly illuminated, turn slowly in the air.

It was a Saturday night, which necessarily meant the cinema for Geneviève and himself. Geneviève sometimes quietly complained that she liked to "entertain". She nursed an unassuaged desire for teas, receptions, "small intimate dinners", that derived from her provincial background. But she knew the horror, "almost unhealthy", she said, that Christophe had for most of his fellow human beings. The crash had rendered the Bohun household empty. Every evening panned out the same way; with the wireless on when Philippe was there, or playing the same records over and again, that Christophe and Murielle loved, till they were half-ruined. But most often, Christophe just paced from one room to another, chain-smoking, and finally muttering:

– I'm going out. I'm going for a short walk, and disappearing.

This evening, at Geneviève's suggestion, they were going on foot as far as the avenue de Wagram. The cinema's facade formed a sparkling block of stark, flashing lights in the humid autumn air.

It was late. The news was over. Almost immediately, Christophe immersed himself in the idiotic bath of well-being, forgetfulness, violent, vague dreaminess, that the cinema alone together with the red burgundy, was capable of procuring. The music was fast and wild.

Rings of smoke, crossed by thin rays of light from the screen, floated slowly in the opaque, stuffy air, lit with a light blue tinge.

A monotonous voice commentated on the pictures:

"The boxing match…"

Two naked fighters were padding in time round a brightly lit ring; one could hear the raucous whistling noise of their breath, and the muffled, low rumble of the crowd. It was happening in America or London, or in Paris… One didn't know, one didn't worry; but those far off shouts and wild breaths mysteriously satisfied the numbed mind. On a racing track in Los Angeles, a car crashed, caught fire; a cloud of smoke and sparks, a man being carried away in haste, who was going to die somewhere, who'd be forgotten; the race wasn't stopped; someone in the room coughed and spoke to his neighbour in a low voice; a woman laughed…How simple everything is…

"What worms we are!", Christophe thought. The drum-rolls, the German soldiers, the peace conference, the Italian soldiers, planes, tanks, artillery:

" Oh, yes, it's true, war…nothing more's needed than all that…Besides, why not?..."

A beautiful peaceful landscape; half-naked men gathered in front of a fire at the side of a lake, surrounded by unknown trees.

– The Islands of the Philippines, said the speaker.

Bright, peaceful, childhood memories rose up; Christophe wanted to hold on for a moment longer to the image of a tree, softly bending in the wind; the mike had captured the light musical rustling of the leaves, moved by a soft spring wind…

But it had already disappeared.

Christophe observed the face of the woman sitting next to him, who had a perfect mouth, beautiful and melancholic. At least it seemed so to him, till in the interval, he saw a made-up girl with heavy features. But he liked the darkness that drowned all the women's faces, and stirred an indefinable feeling in him, violent, sexual, like an unconsummated pleasure.

Interval.

He half-closed his eyes, listened to his neighbours talking. A woman's voice behind him said:

– … With eight hundred francs a month, and life so expensive… How do you expect to get married, Georges? Even if we both work, there'll never be enough… All the same, we have good times as we are, eh? and then, there's also the cinema, a book…Of course it's a pity, but there's nothing we can do about it. Besides, there may be less pleasure, but surely fewer difficulties, it compensates…

– Everything, everything, Christophe thought, was overwhelming: To live, to spend one's unique, short life looking for food, just like a caveman. And even then there must have been good moments, better than today… After a good hunt, lying on the ground…

The interval finished. The American film unfolded in a strange, crazy way. Someone whistled. Others applauded half-heartedly. Most of the faces lifted toward the screen were immobile, indifferent.

Beside him, Geneviève's eyes registered the images of roads and unknown skies, without seeing them. Sometimes she completely closed her eyelids, and the corners of her mouth dropped, the bottom of her cheeks relaxed, giving her a cow-like expression that faintly irritated Christophe.

And, yet, the sounds, the street noises, the general din and shouts of a New York market, took hold of him like some kind of strident, melancholy music, in a way that was both violent and benevolent at the same time.

The lights came on. He got up, cracked his fingers nervously, lit a cigarette. His eyes closed, his eyelids were red and swollen, those around him had tired, inflamed faces, like himself, like escapees from a dream.

For the most part they said:

– What a stupid film.

Then, Christophe and Geneviève went home. The rain had stopped. They retraced their steps on foot. Geneviève yawned quietly, moved nearer her husband, leaned on his arm.

In bed, she extinguished the lamp, turned her body slowly towards him.

He took her in his arms mechanically, and with eyes open in the darkness, focussed on the golden point of a little metal lamp, sometimes touched by the shining rays of a car's headlamp from the street; he gave her the expected usual ration of caresses. Did she feel pleasure?... He had long ago ceased to ask himself … But he kissed her hair with routine politeness.

– Goodnight, my darling…

For a moment, however, he continued caressing it in the dark. The intimate contact softened him.

Then he yawned:

– Goodnight

– Goodnight, she repeated with a little sigh.

After an instant's reflection she added:

– No danger?.. You're sure?...

– What? he murmured mechanically, then:

Oh, yes! … But no, darling, don't worry. I was careful as usual…

Geneviève said in a low voice:

– And yet, I should so much love another child… Well, who knows, later?...

– Yes, of course, said Christophe.

He returned to the remaining cold side of the large bed, with relief. Still a pleasure: sleep…the sheets were fine, slightly used…He stretched out his legs with a feeling of delight.

Both of them remained with their eyes open for a long moment, consciously breathing in a light regular manner that imitated sleep.

Finally, Geneviève fell asleep.

As for Christophe, he tossed and turned in the sheets for a long time, trying to get to sleep. At times he emitted long careworn sighs, as if, in the darkness, he was silently breathing out a deep and incomprehensible pain.

10

Sunday mornings, for Christophe, were spent entirely in an overheated bath, where he marinaded indefinitely, half asleep. He went to see his father. But old James had become sicker; on seeing Christophe he brought his hand up to his throat, tensed his lips and exhaled with a painful grimace:

– Tomorrow!... Leave me in peace…

After lunch, Christophe went to find the car. The All Saints Day holiday was beginning, but the cold, at this time of the year, was more biting than usual. Women dressed in mourning went past, their arms full of flowers; the wind blew the long black veils that hung from the widows' hair forcefully, and rustled the chrysanthemums lying in the carts.

Christophe drove haphazardly toward one of Paris's gates. He wasn't thinking about anything. He didn't know where he was going, he didn't want to know. Eyes fixed on the horizon, lips trembling, he was waiting, for a swig of alcohol, for the first breath of fresh air – all else aside, the one and only pleasure in life. For him, perhaps, the special moment when he downed champagne in an obscure bar, when he felt alive and nearly happy. He looked forward to these Sundays with so much impatience, such anticipation, and how rare they seemed…sometimes he had to lend the car to Philippe and sometimes Geneviève came with him. That, that was the worst… As soon as it got dark on the deserted winter roads, she began to comment nervously:

– Careful, careful Christophe…

Then:

– Put the windows up...The wind's blowing in your back, my darling, be careful, you had a sore throat, yesterday...

And inevitably coming back to:

– What's this?...Have you got the map?...What's this village we've just been through called?... Are you sure, at least, we're on the right road?...

How he, himself, loved to travel spontaneously, on an unmade badly lit road. It wasn't the speed he liked in a car...like some others...Besides the little Renault didn't lend itself to that... No, it was something else... The solitude, the silence of the countryside, the sky, the wind...

In the past, Murielle had come with him whatever the time; they would drive the whole night long to see the sun come up over the sea, in autumn. In the past...

But that was all gone. Murielle was nearly an old woman now, and petrol was expensive.

– The only happiness that God's given to man, Christophe repeated to himself with a kind of desperate love, stroking the side of the car with his hand. It was hot and trembling like a horse's body. When he was alone, like today, he didn't worry about being on a good road, he took the smallest side roads, the most isolated. It was already winter in this cold countryside. He saw a pool covered with a dark crust of frost, where in places silvery black ice shone through. The bare trees bent over, shaken by a strong wind. The horizon was vast and deep; in the forbidding, desperate, grey sky, clouds were coming in waves from the North. Some heavy grey ones went past, under a flock of black birds.

Christophe slowed down gradually and stopped. He leaned his head toward the lowered window, and breathed in with all his soul, the smell of the earth and the rotting leaves.

A light layer of creaking ice remained intact on the rut made by the wheels. Suddenly he felt impelled to get out. With keen, child-like pleasure, he gave it a mighty heel-kick, causing silvery shards of broken crystal to go flying. Then he stayed, immobile, bare-headed, eyes closed, letting the wind gust and whistle around him, savouring the icy tears running down his cheeks with an inexplicable delight.

He got back in the car. Not a soul. Just a racing car that overtook him, blue and steel, its voracious bonnet, streamlined like a pike's snout, directed towards empty space. The low sky deposited some little drops on the windscreen, which the wind sent running in all directions. The road was grey and slippery. Night was falling. These gloomy autumn sunsets were the best thing in the world. One saw nothing but black and grey throughout the countryside. The tree-branches dropped a little rain, fine and cold. A cart went past, its tarpaulin shining with rain, and everywhere for miles around, was just solitude, space and silence. He drove through a village at very slow speed, looking with an obscure, violent curiosity at the small low houses with lighted windows. The sort of people who lived there, whoever they were, whatever miserable tramps, seemed preferable to himself.

– Why am I so unhappy, after all? He murmured, nearly out loud: Lost childhood?...

He remembered his mother, her blond curls, her hard made-up face, her cold eyes... For him, she had been one of the shameful things of childhood, an absence one divulges to nobody and keeps locked up in the bottom of one's heart, whose bitterness one never stops ruminating over, until the day one dies.

– No... It's not that...That was so long ago... Father?...That horrible monetary tyranny, which weighed down my childhood, that dependence on money, which has stifled me all my life and which still overwhelms me, like a kind of congenital curse... I was better off during the war. Life, at least, seemed to have a value. Now...Ah! I don't know, but it's monstrous to be my age and to be so weary, so indifferent to everything, so dried up and lacking in love...In the end, life's the same for everyone... And others, how do they do it? They get used to it. They accept it. But I'm one of the lucky ones in this world, and the man who went by in his cart, under the soaking tarpaulin, should have the right to look at me with envy!... I'm young, healthy, I know all that, and if somebody said: "You're going to die tomorrow!" I wouldn't have a minute's regret. I don't love life. Speaking of love, the only good thing is physical. I wish I was an animal, a plant, a stone. Shitty life, shitty life, he repeated with brooding concentration, his eye fixed continuously on the road which was becoming impossible to see, melding with the black bushes on either side.

He waited, he didn't put on headlights; he enjoyed the obscurity, the rain, the wind that lashed his face, the little greyish puddles full of ice, that shone in the night. He began to feel his shoulders getting numbed by the air, which was becoming increasingly sharp and icy. He drove through a small dark village, where one could see, vaguely in the shadows, a fountain in the middle of a square and bare plane trees. The half-open door of a wine bar, gave out warm air and a red light. Next to it was parked, between two old marker-posts, the blue and steel racing car which had overtaken him in the mist on the road.

He got down and went in, and the first face he saw was that of his son.

The small narrow room was feebly lit by gas lamps, hanging above a zinc counter. Philippe was sitting at a wooden table, between an unknown man and woman, drinking a grog; the steaming glasses filled the air with bluish vapour, a penetrating odour of alcohol and fire.

As usual, Philippe affected an unruffled, unbothered by anything air; slowly got up from his chair, held out two fingers to his father and said between his teeth:

– I thought it was your car we passed…You don't drive fast, you're a *good boy*…Papa, don't you recognise your cousin Pena?…he added.

– Ah, yes, murmured Christophe, frowning.

Christophe hadn't seen Pena, Murielle's husband, for many years, since the time when Murielle and he separated.

He was a tall thin man, who strikingly resembled the king of Spain; he accentuated the resemblance by holding his neck up straight in a rigid manner, as if it was supported by an iron collar; his thick lip was surmounted by a small light moustache, 1900 style, which was beginning to whiten; his eyes, small, deep-set, had a fixed ironic look and the dilated pupils of the inebriated.

The woman who accompanied him, a thin girl with heavily made up cheekbones, never took her eyes off Philippe.

Christophe sighed involuntarily, the sight of his cousin stirred irksome old memories…

They exchanged some awkward words:

– It's a long time since we met…

And some others.

Then, they became quiet. Christophe was sitting next to Pena, who smoked silently looking up at him from time to time. Eventually he asked:

– It's all the same to you if I sometimes take the lad?…

Christophe shrugged his shoulders:

– Of course…

He contemplated the yellowed face, with the thick pendulous lower lip. That man had always had the mark of a renegade, a gigolo… no matter he came from a good Spanish family, and was vaguely related to Christophe's mother. He seemed to have aged and quietened down; his youth had been stormy. As if he'd guessed Christophe's thoughts, Pena said:

– Nowadays I'm selling racing cars, privately, on behalf of an Italian firm… "Greatness and decadence" seems to be the family motto. I'm in Paris for a while, only, for the Salon…

He hesitated, lowered his voice imperceptibly and asked:

– How's Murielle?

He went pale, the fingers holding his cigarette, trembled, when he pronounced the name.

– Well, said Christophe, dryly.

It pained him that Pena took such trouble to speak of Murielle… But why, the pain?… he thought with irritation. After all, if he wants her back… if she, at least, were to consent… that'd be better, perhaps, for all concerned…

Pena, for his part, looked at him with a strange insistence:

– So much water's gone under the bridge since…

He indicated Philippe:

– A man, now… and we're, finished old man…I envy you having a son…If I'd had a son, everything would've been different, he said, and abruptly became silent.

– One believes so, Christophe murmured lazily.

– Listen, papa, said Philippe, getting up.

He went towards the corner of the bistro and set in motion an ancient music box. Some notes were missing. The low muffled sounds of an old waltz filtered through the air.

– I miss her, Pena suddenly said with effort, that's reasonable isn't it?

His dilated pupil fixed the kind of look on Christophe that made him think: "He still loves her, he's still jealous, my word…"

– So cold, said the woman who accompanied Paco.

– So cold, they repeated lazily, one after the other.

A small stove was burning next to them. Christophe mechanically turned the handle. A blast of heat escaped from it, with a red flame.

– Where did you come from? Christophe asked.

He didn't listen to the response.

– But where are we here? he said after a moment.

– Bonneville.

The music stopped. Christophe murmured:

– Another one.

– It's late, Pena said, we're going back. Are you coming with? Are you warmed up now?

– Not yet, Christophe murmured. I'll stay here. Good-bye.

11

Alone, Christophe got up from the table, walked lazily toward the music box, turned the heavy handle with an effort. Once again, the muffled, croaky notes spread out slowly, falling, one by one, like drops of water, in the silence. The workers rubbed their lime-coated jacket-sleeves on the zinc counter, drinking silently. Like them, Christophe was leaning on it, looking fixedly at the small low window, on the other side of which a lantern burnt feebly in the shadows and the rain. A grey fountain was illuminated by a dull, blurred light, the kind one sees in dreams.

The past…

– It's funny, he thought, you live side by side and you end up forgetting the past…so completely… Love?... What a meaningless word, as the years go by, how they envelope the heart with their thickness, their weight…Beautiful love…I've even forgotten her body, her face, from the past…

He interrupted himself, lowered his head. The image of the woman as she was in the present, effaced the memory of the beautiful young girl, whose first lover he had been. Murielle, today… Murielle, sitting in front of the fire, leaning her head forward, faded eyes, heavy eyelids…

– She loved me, she gave herself to me, even though still a child, knowing full well, he thought confusedly, that I'd bring her nothing but misfortune…

It's probably because of me and my marriage that she married Pena, my fault that she separated from him, that she came back to live with us. Now...she's still absolutely mine, at my disposition... I know, only too well...She doesn't have any illusions about me, yet, God knows... She knows me well enough... Yet, she's always looked on the dark side, been a pessimist, wearisome... But proud in her own way, and secretive, giving everything without ever stooping to make any demands... Even now, she could try to recover the past, with memories, words... But no... And as soon as I began to detach myself from her, she was the first to untie the knot that bound us together...already so loose.

For a moment he saw her mouth again. She was so beautiful, still, that mouth, with the turned down corners, whose lips seemed chiselled and edges deeply hollowed...That sad, fine mouth in an aging face...

– No, he thought, she can't blame me. It's not my fault. I've no more love in my heart...What a time, my God, to think of these things...a caricature of youth, of the past, of love? No, no, no!...I'm tired, I'm warn out, life is too hard, too difficult...You have to have your head and your heart free, to think of love... Love?... What nonsense...

He half-closed his eyes, murmured with a lazy harshness:

– To hell with memories...

He paid, went back to Paris.

The tyres skidded on the wet road. The wind had dropped.

In Paris, he parked his car and walked the streets for a long time before returning home. Along the way the red doors of wine-bars opened. Christophe looked at the women coming out, most were so ugly that the sight of their faces extinguished his vague desire.

He walked randomly, letting the rain wet his cheeks with a feeling of pleasure. In the darkness, he no longer recognised the streets, but he kept his eyes down on purpose in the obscurity, he wasn't looking for street names in the shadow of the tall buildings. He walked, as if in an unknown city, whistling to himself, looking round with curiosity. Several shops were still open despite it being Sunday, and the late hour.

He passed by a brightly lit dairy, situated between two enormous wickerwork baskets, full to the brim with white eggs, lit by a garland of bare lights.

Two women bumped into him. They were laughing and talking to one another. The voice of one of them struck him:

– I like those flash-tails' voices, he thought confusedly, they're like the music in the bistro… saturated in alcohol, with missing notes …

A shiver of pleasure ran through his flesh. He quickened his pace, overtook the two women. One was old, but the other had a young face, made up, with long dark eyebrows. Christophe took her arm abruptly, whispered some words in her ear. She laughed, let herself be taken. Love's only pleasure…

12

When Christophe got back to the house, Geneviève was asleep. He was crossing the large drawing room to join her, when he noticed Murielle, sitting in front of the fire, reading. The room was plunged in darkness, and she didn't see him coming. She held the poker in her hand, shoving piles of coke around at regular intervals. A red flame rose and lit up her face.

She leaned her head forward; her short hair, still healthy and luxuriant, was permed in tight waves, hanging in tresses; her neck, which supported her weary face like a collar, pure and strong as a column in the past, was hollowed out by three concentric lines; she had wrapped it and her shoulders in a green silk shawl, which only allowed the bottom of her black dress to be seen; she was smoking, mechanically shaking the cigarette ash into the fire; the smoke swirled around her lowered head, slowly rose toward the high painted ceiling.

At the sound of footsteps on the floor, she turned around and stared at Christophe without speaking to him or smiling.

– Cold as a bitch, he said distractedly, and he approached the fire, holding both his hands to the flames and slowly withdrawing them, rubbing them together.

– Where's Geneviève?

She made a vague sign with her head toward the neighbouring bedroom. She lowered her face toward her book again. While reading she kept pulling her wedding ring to the end of her finger and letting it drop onto the pages. She gathered it up automatically, slid it back onto her finger, and began again.

He had his back to the window and was watching the changes in her face, her hair, which hadn't whitened but reddened in places like a used fur.

Murielle got up abruptly, and before he could stop her, passed in front of him with one of those light ethereal movements that she'd preserved, in contrast to her increasingly weighty body. She drew the lace curtain, mended skilfully enough by Geneviève, but seeming, like everything else in this dark room, dilapidated and strange. Then, she pushed another armchair in front of the fire and said to Christophe:

– Don't look at me like that… It exasperates me… Sit down and keep quiet.

– You prefer this room to the little sitting room? he asked mechanically.

– Yes, there's never anybody here. And my bedroom's really too cold.

He suppressed a weary laugh.

– Excuse me…But can I stay?...

– Of course, she murmured, shrugging her shoulders.

They became silent. The fire was going down. Only one red hot coal remained in the grate. Christophe watched the reflections from the flames play upon the marble fireplace in a sort of stupor.

– I wonder, he suddenly thought, if she looks back, like me?...

He interrupted himself. The past... He'd never worried about it.

– It's that idiot Pena's fault, he thought angrily. The past... Childhood... He had lived his whole life side by side with Murielle, an orphan, taken in by old James. How beautiful she'd been... He remembered that night, before the war, when he'd come home in the early hours of the morning with her...They'd come back from a ball...They came into this very room, which had certainly changed, she also, my God...Warm, luxurious, with crackling wood fires, that Bohun loved, kept going all night for him...flames dancing on the tapestries, the old furniture, the flowers... It was a spring night in 1912. At that time one could still hear the sound of horses' hooves on the wooden pavement. Those pretty flowers in the vases, remembering that night it still seemed to him he could recognise the sweet, the dangerous perfume. She had run to the window. And it was here, at this very window, with this same, sad, green, gas lamp, in the shadows, that he had kissed her for the first time. He had always been rough and hurried in love, his fingers squeezing her breasts, pressing a breathless mouth... But she was such a beauty, that night in may, that fresh skin, smooth and slippery under his teeth, the ball-gown, thrown on a chair, that white muslin, trodden and crumpled by himself, the joyful flowers, the springtime, the light wind blowing through the open window...He seemed to feel the trembling in his body again, that delicious tiredness. He sighed profoundly.

In 1914, he had enlisted. A little later he'd met Geneviève. At that time, it seemed to him that only a simple, pure woman like her, would be able to sooth him, efface the memories of the front. He'd got married, and Murielle had married Paco.

After a short while, the whole thing started up again. But love was already different; for him, at least... it had lost its flavour, its scent of freedom and youthfulness; it was no more than a silent bedding, an impassioned bitter feeling, torturous and trivial at the same time, troubled by the first money worries and the stifled remorse in the face of Geneviève, so mysteriously impenetrable...

Finally, in 1924, the crash had supervened. Love?... Time enough...The ties were gently unknotted, without disturbance and without words. Both of them hated words. At present the life he led only left room for brutal desire, quickly satisfied.

– To wait, to lie, to caress, how tiresome...

It's not worth the trouble... Love, pleasure, it's such a small thing...

He let a little painful laugh escape.

– You seem to be in a particularly black humour tonight, she said at last.

He shook his head without replying.

– Is it true, she asked in an undertone, that you met Paco?

– Yes. Did Philippe tell you?

– He's changed. He seemed wearier, more sensible.

– So have you seen him again? said Christophe with a quick movement that he wasn't able to suppress.

– No. He wrote to me several times. He wanted me to come back. I remembered the past. The gambling, the drugs... Never any money, living like a king, and the suppliers coming to the office, wanting to be paid... But all that seems so far away...Perhaps, in the end, it'd be the best thing. But what frightens me is moving. I'd like to stay in the same place till I die. I'm tired, tired...

– You sleep instead of living, he said.

– So do you, so do you, come...

– Why does one go on living? he murmured.

– Out of habit, I suppose.

They became quiet again. In the neighbouring dining-room, the house-keeper, a heavy Luxembourgian, went slowly back and forth to the dessert table. The parquet floor was old and creaked under her feet. Each time she got near the door of the room she had to tread very lightly, and one could hear the rising floor-boards make a furtive little groan, which added to the atmosphere of night and silence. It was nearly eleven o'clock and Christophe felt his eyelids getting heavy.

– Tomorrow, the office.

She looked at him, astonished by his violent tone of voice.

A sort of howl escaped from him.

– The office!... Beryl's ugly mug... The bar... dinner...Saturday cinema... The car, and the whore picked up in the street, Sunday night...Week after week, the same thing, unto death! How I hate this life!...

– What do you want? she said in a low voice.

– A human existence that isn't completely eaten up by worrying about money, daily bread and work!... There are some rainy mornings when I leave the house and want to lie down in the middle of the road, and wait for the first bus to come along and run me over. It's stupid, isn't it? These lamentations!, more like Philippe's kind of thing... I'm like those idealistic young people who went to Tahiti after the war!...

– You, she said in an ironic tone, you wouldn't be happy in Tahiti. They don't have any bathrooms.

– That's only too true. Lost children of capitalism that we are!... I've missed out on everything, since this life is all about getting hold of money, everything's taken away from you... Perhaps others find it... a higher goal... But I'm desperately average, the man in the street, it's not my fault...

– Yes, she said.

Suddenly it came to him that her life was even more gloomy and monotonous than his own. He asked with a strange effort:

– But Murielle, what do you do, you, all day long?

– I don't know. I'm waiting to die.

She knocked the ash from her cigarette into the fire, and finished lightly:

– Like you. Like everyone over the age of twenty...

– It's a normal occupation, for all human beings. I've nothing against it. Death, renunciation, old age, I accept it, I'm resigned. I hate what life's done to me. I get up, I wait for the time to go to the office, and when I'm there, I wait for the time to leave. And, in general, I wait for the end of the month.

– And uncle James's death, she said quietly.

He shivered:

– I know. I hate myself, you hear, I detest myself.

– That's odd.

– What?

– You never said…

He shrugged his shoulders violently.

– And who should I have said it to? Geneviève?

She said nothing. He thought:

– This is the real Murielle, the Murielle of the past…It's a rare woman who isn't upset by a rival, even after so many years…But she's always been like that…

He looked at her coldly, curiously. He thought of her body, without desire, which had gained weight round the chest and hips. Only her voice and the form of her mouth were delightful. Yet an obscure heat ran in his veins. He stretched out his hand, stroked the shawl softly, twisted the fringe around his fingers, gently took the wedding ring that she'd allowed to roll along her skirt and which was still warm from contact with her hands, let it fall with a little sigh. She didn't remove it; he distinctly perceived a little shiver run through her.

Nearly an hour went by. Neither of them spoke. They watched the fire burn in the dark room, drowned in a deep melancholy dreaminess…

13

One evening, sometime before the Christmas holidays, Christophe was at the bar; clients at that time were few and far between, saving their money for Christmas boxes and the end of the year; occasionally a fat business-man, arms full of parcels with dolls' hair hanging out of them, the box for a drum, came in and downed a glass without sitting, then left. A woman whom Christophe had seen several times over the course of the years, who disappeared and reappeared unpredictably, was sitting on a bar-stool for hours, sadly shaking her cigarette ash into an empty glass. She had a hoarse voice, bruised painted cheeks, dyed hair that showed under her black hat, warn out shoes and a weak, blasé smile fixed on her face.

Some men who knew her grinned and called her *Card Trick*. Several nights in a row, she chose to sit on the stool next to Christophe, but she soon understood that any effort in his direction would be useless. However he bought her a drink, and treated her with the ceremonious courtesy he reserved especially for down and out whores.

So, on this particular evening, after having shared his bottle of champagne, she sighed and said:

– You're a smart guy… no fooling with women. It's rare, and I should know. You remind me of a man I once had, an Englishman.

– Oh! Christophe said distractedly.

He spent six or seven months of the year cruising a yacht and the rest of the time he was in one country or another. He was a bit of a nut. He had a house in every country that he liked, one in Coïmbre, another in Norway, yet another in Florence. They were all furnished, servants in each of them; he'd arrive there, stay for a month or six weeks, then leave, spend entire seasons on the sea, alone, or with some women that he picked up here and there, in a bar, or a port, and dropped equally quickly... He liked me, he kept me longer than the others, but I was young, and got bored... You understand, one's young, solitude's very beautiful, but it's annoying after a while, no? she said laughing, and Panam', I missed Panam', the cinemas and all the rest...Would you like that, that kind of life? she said suddenly, lightly caressing Christophe's hand by force of habit, I can see it in your eyes.

– Yes, he murmured.

He powerfully imagined the white bridge of a yacht, covered in salt and spray. Sailing freely on a limitless sea, stopping by chance, according to his whim of the moment, in an unknown country, nothing else to do in the world but dream, bathe in the sea, watch the sun shining on the waves, on the far off towns, to be alive at last, to live!...

He vaguely heard the woman speaking:

– You can imagine what a colossal fortune you need to live that way...

– That's true, always the same thing, he thought, coming back to his senses. Whichever way you look, always this cursed money. You need billions to live that way. Damnation! Did she really need to tell me about all that!...

– Me, now that I'm older and I know life better, I think a man like that, if I'd known how to handle him, I could have done whatever I wanted. You know a normal man gets tired at the end of this life. It's good for society, isn't it? one needs society and civilisation above all. What do you think?

– Oh! Of course, Christophe said.

The woman spoke a while more; she was a bit drunk and shook her powder-puff randomly about her face, and in her glass. Without listening to her, Christophe was watching confused images of sails, masts, and brilliant suns, pass across the dark wall of the smoke-filled bar.

– And what happened to him in the end, your friend? he asked.

– Him? Didn't I tell you? He died mad.

Christophe laughed cheerlessly.

– So much the better!... That proves that it's impossible to be completely happy down here, and that's a consolation for poor guys like us! The new proletarians!

– Ah! the woman said, in a sentimental tone, was he so happy? Perhaps he'd never known true love!... Life, even the most magnificent, is only worthwhile with love!...

– Just so, Christophe replied.

14

In the Bohun household, Christmas brought sprigs of mistletoe over the doors every year and holly in the vases, rum pudding made by Geneviève.

During dinner, the telephone rang continuously, and every time a woman's voice asked:

– Is M. Philippe Bohun there?

– Go on, darling, it's OK for tonight, Geneviève said to her son.

He got up, took the telephone into his bedroom, and his parents heard through the wall:

– H'm!... Yes... Even you, old man... I'll be free right away... What?... Oh! always the same thing... Yes, it's annoying but there's nothing one can do... We're going to Jim's this evening?... It'll be awful, probably, but where would you want to go when there's no dosh?... After?... Well, Montparnasse, some club, wherever...

– Wherever, Christophe thought: wherever, away from the house, parents, worries, money and illness...How I understand him...

And Philippe, having swallowed the last mouthful, looked at his watch, waited for nearly an hour, red-cheeked, eyes lit up with a dark fire, then disappeared.

The warm glow produced by the punch died away. Everyone stood in front of the fireplace, empty-handed. The room seemed colder and larger than ever. Silence fell again. Time went by. Outside, one could hear the taxis, the shouts of late night revellers, hurried footsteps on the pavements, muffled party sounds, joyful and confused. The porte cochère was opening and closing all the time; voices and laughter could be heard on the stairs and in the courtyard. Gramophones and wirelesses let rip in the neighbouring apartments, all playing different tunes at the same time, melting together in an indistinct cacophony. Above the Bohun's they were dancing. The rhythm of people's feet could be heard pounding on the floor accompanied by a brouhaha of laughs and cries. A little decorated Christmas tree allowed its pink candles to melt, sadly, on the window-sill. Geneviève thought about Philippe's childhood and her own. Courtenay... the modern cold little church and the smell and smoke of incense... Courtenay had been built not far from the sea. The air there was mild and humid, blown by gusts of warm wind; a taste of salt remained on the lips. She used to go to church willingly in those days, but she hated the cold, she was on her own. Back there, her sister and cousins were, doubtless, eating their Christmas dinner at this very moment. Indistinct, far off images of childhood, formed in the depths of her memory. Christmas and New Year's eve, everyone reviewed their lives. What was she doing here, in this alienating environment, where nothing seemed in place, neither objects nor people?... She murmured:

– The pudding wasn't as good as usual.

– But of course it was, my darling, said Christophe.

– I found it excellent.

Murielle made an effort to keep the conversation going and hazarded:

– The pastry was a bit too heavy, perhaps…

– Oh no, said Geneviève in a scornful and indulgent tone, what an idea, darling!... There just wasn't enough sugar…

Murielle became silent. Every now and again she looked at Christophe, lips mute, beautiful hands abandoned on her knees; a bitter mocking little contraction passed across her features. She still held a flame…

On his own, during these evenings, Christophe didn't think about anything. He had long ago passed through the stage of memories. He was cold and thirsty. At one o'clock Geneviève went to bed. Murielle remained on her own smoking, in front of an open book that she wasn't reading. Christophe went out, went to a little English bar that he knew, where they drew Christmas raffles, and had a lit up Christmas tree standing between the counter and the tables. A sad old negro that the northern rains seemed to have washed out, stained a coffee-brown colour mixed with water, was singing in a low voice, sitting in a corner, head inclined to one side, eyes half-closed. There weren't many women, but some ponderous drunken Englishmen, who were giving people slaps on the back, a brouhaha of "cheer-ee-oo", "Have a good Christmas", "Cheer up", that lasted until morning. The ice-cold champagne caused a liquid fire to run in his veins which kept on burning; the tree began to spin in front of Christophe's weary eyes. He went home slowly along the shining, dark streets, full of sleet.

Tramps were silently hanging around the walls. From time to time, he ran into a group of large men in cloaks, with pink paper hats on their heads, holding unkempt women by the arm, the ends of streamers hooked onto their furs, their make-up running softly under the morning rain; he heard:

" We're drunk, but so what!... We've had a good laugh...You have to laugh once a year... Work, tomorrow... But hey, at least we've had a good laugh..."

That particular year, he seemed more irritable and anxious than ever, less resigned to the depressing solitary festival. And the weather wasn't the same as in previous years. The clouds and ice had begun earlier than usual, preceded by a week of cold and dark, of brilliant shadows out of which shone the shop lights, sparkling like icy tears. A real snow was falling, thick and fast. Yet, scarcely had it landed, than it began to melt, changing itself into grey trickles of semi-frozen mud, slippery under foot. One evening, when he got back from the office, Christophe and his wife met under the arch of the porte cochère. Geneviève was hurrying; the cold had reddened her cheeks; flakes of snow were spread all over her hair and little black hat, that made her look very alluring.

Christophe suddenly said:

– If you like, darling, we could take the car and spend a couple of days in the country.

– Where would we go?

He shrugged his shoulders:

– Anywhere...

Geneviève looked at the night striped with snow-flakes, sighing gently.

– It's not a bad idea...

They went up together in the lift, an ancient machine that ascended slowly in the air, grinding and groaning.

We could take Murielle with us, Christophe said suddenly.

And immediately he thought angrily:

– I'm sick?... Why am I going to burden myself with these two women?...

But Geneviève said:

– Certainly, darling…

15

They left the following day, so early that the snow which had fallen during the night was still lying undisturbed on the roads. The weather was particularly beautiful and icy; gentle pink rays of light lit the houses. In the country, trees powdered with snow reflected a delightful pale light.

The car rumbled along, skidding from time to time on the frost-coated roads. The two women at the back of the vehicle, spoke to each other in undertones in a routine kind of exchange.

Christophe wasn't thinking of anything; he felt happy and relaxed. The sun was shining; fine snow fell like sugar sprinkled over the gentle hills and woods that formed the undulating landscape in that part of the world. In some places, marshes or lakes covered with a carapace of ice were sparkling.

After Avallon, the weather changed. The sun went in, and a grey mist gradually covered the horizon. Snow began to fall, in a blinding, gloomy storm that impaired visibility.

In a small town, whose name none of them knew, they stopped in front of an inn.

The roads were deserted. A lone horse hitched to a cart in the middle of the carriageway, was snorting steam out of its nostrils; it was the only sound that disturbed the silence other than that of its hooves tapping the ground.

While the women drank hot tea in the lower room, Christophe went outside and breathed in the evening mist for some time. The snow was turning into a thick blanket of fog, through which an occasional light shone.

He approached a house built a little away from the carriageway on the corner of the road, a simple, grey, provincial house, with small, covered, faintly lit windows. Through the closed shutters, one could see a yellow fire burning at the back of the room. Putting his hand to his ear, Christophe thought he could hear the gentle crackling of the logs.

He sighed:

– What peace…

A hand inside the house lowered a curtain, and the light went out. But Christophe remained motionless, frowning.

– I think I'd like that kind of life, he thought confusedly, a slow life, peaceful, measured by the passage of the seasons, harmonious, without regrets or desires. Yet, what do I know about it?... No doubt life's equally hard everywhere. Courtenay, for example, horrible!...

Christophe walked slowly toward the church tower, scarcely visible, blurred in the fog. A clock began to strike; he waited till it had struck four times, each one accompanied by a sort of little jingling sound, light and musical, fine and ironic, like a woman's laugh.

Gently, hesitantly, he stretched out his hand and touched the cold stones; he repeated with a heavy heart:

– What peace…

Then he felt cold and went back.

Murielle and Geneviève were still talking to one another, in that easy, friendly tone, which members of the same family use in a familiar, conspiratorial kind of way, that rapid shorthand way of mentioning events and judging people.

Christophe sat down in front of them, joked and laughed; he felt strangely at ease, with an empty, light heart. They, who in Paris only talked about very specific things, dresses, money worries, or health; were suddenly exchanging half-confidences, sad, vain fantasies.

– I only want peace, Murielle said in an undertone, and since we have to grow old, let it begin, let it happen quickly, finally… completely… It's like death. Getting there is the hardest. Once it's done…

– Me, said Geneviève, but she sighed and became quiet.

– Security, without doubt, Christophe thought, money, naturally, in order not to have to worry, or wait anxiously for the next day, to no longer have to count my father's coughing fits in the middle of the night. It's strange, Geneviève herself, the calm one, isn't really satisfied with life, she who could have lived so happy and fulfilled, with so little money… Why the devil did she marry me? And myself?... Could anyone think of a marriage so badly matched, so stupid?... Does she see it the same way?...

He shook his head abruptly:

– What's the good of thinking about all that, good God?

– Let's go, he said in a loud voice, it's late.

Murielle and he stopped for a moment to pick up the menus that had fallen down. Murielle stubbed her cigarette on the wooden table; some ash detached itself and dropped off; a spark flew out; she watched it burn for a second and then go out.

– And you, Christophe? she murmured involuntarily.

He clenched his teeth with a dry, savage little laugh:

– Too long, it'd take too long to explain...

He looked at her more closely, and a sudden heat rose into his temples:

– What I want more than anything? At this moment?... You, perhaps...

She lowered her head without replying; he took her arm, escorted her to the car. They left.

Night fell very early. They were driving between some bare trees that seemed to clutch and rub one another, to overlap their dry branches under a dismal sky. The snow fell ceaselessly.

Christophe entered into a passionate and confused reverie. He had forgotten the women, silent now, in the lit up car. Murielle was smoking. Every now and then, Geneviève wiped the iced up window with the back of her glove, asking:

– Where are we?

He didn't reply. He breathed in the fog and the dark night. From time to time, feeling smothered, he lowered the window and leaned outside, his face on fire. The snow and wind playing on the peaceful countryside, were transforming it into a bleak, savage land. They arrived very late at a small hotel by the side of a river; the headlights lit up the heavy glistening waters. They dined. Geneviève was tired. She looked at the many couples around them, and every now and then, turned to Murielle saying animatedly but in an undertone:

– Look, darling, that woman sitting there, on your left... Her hat looks like mine, the black, don't you think? Truly, I don't know what to wear. In Paris, we don't go anywhere, we don't see anything, she continued in a tone of gentle resignation, which gradually became more and more embittered, like milk souring with age, but as Christophe was still listening, she added in a tender ironic tone: my poor dear, we live like savages...

But this evening, Christophe only had eyes for Murielle. He had drunk a lot. He poured some wine into the ladies' glasses. Geneviève said reproachfully:

– Christophe... be careful of your liver, my darling...

Murielle drank silently becoming more and more pale and silent. Her eyes burned with a strange mournful fire; two red patches lit up her cheeks, a little nervous tremor agitated her hands.

For the first time in many long years, Murielle's love, which normally evoked nothing in him but a dull sense of remorse and irritation, brought the unextinguished past back to life in Christophe's heart. And as soon as he felt touched by desire, he became happy. He forced himself to look at her, to remember her body. For a moment, he thought that nothing had ever seemed so sensual, so desirable, as those two fiery patches on her pale cheeks. At other times, when she turned her head and he noticed the fine lines in the corner of her eyes, under the make-up, he thought ironically:

– How one day at the office, Beryl had said: "There's no rise in the markets...there couldn't be a rise in 1934... it's a fluctuation, it doesn't mean a thing..." My God, this seems the same... How I'd like to reignite love in myself, one day, just for an hour, to have something else in my thoughts other than the daily grind, but " it's a fluctuation, it doesn't mean a thing..." But I did love her, he thought with a suppressed voluptuousness, strange and painful, I loved her...

Dinner finished. They retired to their bedrooms.

Christophe remained standing in front of the open window for some time, breathing the cold air saturated with moisture. Opposite him a green lantern gave off a deep, steady light that didn't illuminate the night, but made it seem even darker and more opaque. The snow stopped, then started to fall again more slowly; the occasional silver flake flew obliquely, blown by the wind toward the open window.

He hovered for a moment. To start all over again?... What stupidity... And yet... He ran his hand several times across his boiling forehead, then closed the window bolts, quietly went down the corridor; in Genevieve's bedroom, beside his own, the light was already out; he opened Murielle's door. She was in bed, but not asleep, motionless, her head thrown backward on the cushions. Tears were glowing in her open eyes.

Christophe sat down on the bed, grabbed her breasts with a sudden ferocity that astonished himself. She said absolutely nothing; a sort of light grimace of sufferance half-opened her lips, she gave a sigh and fell back on the bed.

When he withdrew, she stayed lying down, forehead pressed into the cushion. She said in a stifled voice:

– Not tomorrow, I suppose?

He shivered lightly, coming to his senses, empty of desire. He murmured sadly:

– Tomorrow, Murielle, I'll be a different man… bitter, exhausted,… mentally sick… It's not my fault… But I can't offer you more than this… one night, from time to time, when I feel the need…

She didn't reply, took another of her eternal cigarettes, lit it, watched the smoke, fixedly. Then she turned away in order not to have to see Christophe, his tall body inclined toward the bed, the wild movement of his tense lips.

– Leave me…

A green light shone in the black window. In the silence of the little provincial hotel, they distinctly heard the hour chime, an alarm-clock went off in a distant bedroom. The time to think of love had passed…

She forced herself to look at Christophe through her tears, sitting on the bed, smoking, head thrown back, her face was weary and bitter, her eyes ringed.

She murmured with a profound sense of lassitude:

– Go now…

Christophe silently kissed her naked shoulder and went back to his own room.

16

The first Saturday of the year, having accomplished all the rites for this day of the week (hair, manicure, bar…), Christophe returned home. He encountered Murielle on the doorstep; silently took her hand and carried her away.

They walked for a while in the streets, jostled by passers-by; all the faces they met wore the same bad-tempered expression on their features, which marks the crowd after the Christmas respite, when worries that had been deliberately put aside for forty-eight hours, seem once again to fall with their full weight on people's shoulders.

Murielle stopped.

– I'm tired , she said without looking at him.

She turned her face away, biting her lips with an irresolute, nervous expression.

For a moment he thought about an hotel, but almost immediately an abrupt wave of irritation and despair extinguished the brief flame of desire.

– Let's cross the road…

He took her in to a little chauffeurs' and coach-drivers' bistro, where he sometimes bought stamps. They sat down behind a wooden partition on a worn bench. The place was smoky and noisy, but the room was huge, with high ceilings supported by blackened beams, giving an overwhelming impression of space. They ordered a drink at random, and remained seated without speaking.

– Love? Christophe mused one more time. Yes, that'd be good, if it didn't entail so much talking, caressing and lying… It all bores me to death. I

want to leave. Alone, above all, good God, alone!...
As soon as one puts out one's neck, one can feel the
chain. Miserable dogs that we are... I want to live,
simply to live, and not work. Doubtless, every
human being in the world, since the beginning of
time, has dreamed of happiness without worries,
witness the Garden of Eden. And, certainly, one
can't avoid old age, sickness, death; but work, at
least, the curse of work we could be saved from...
I'm not thinking of the work of a doctor, a
peasant... but people like me, the majority, the little
ones, the small people on a monthly salary!... To
work, to give everything that makes life worth
while, dreams, leisure, even the air and God's own
light, in exchange for your daily bread, and not
even that's assured... So go and make love under
those conditions...

– If I was rich, he said in a loud voice, this could
continue, but as things are, it'd be better to finish
once and for all and forget. We've been good for a
long time. If I was rich...

She paled a little:

– I can't see well, she murmured.

He indicated the smoke-filled room.

– Ideal décor...

He reflected and added, shrugging his shoulders:

– And in the house it'd be worse...

She slowly stubbed out her cigarette against the
marble table, where the dark trace of her glass
remained.

– Perhaps...

However, recriminations, vain complaints
mounted to his lips, in spite of everything. She

became quiet. He took her hand, carried it to his face, placed his cheek against the trembling fingers, covered up his bitter, melancholic smile in a kiss.

– My poor Murielle…

He whistled softly:

No more money in the bank
No cute baby we can spank
Oh, what to do?…

She got up abruptly. He shrugged his shoulders, paid, and they went back together, without speaking, along the black roads.

17

That night, Christophe, who was sleeping particularly deeply, heard a hurried, whispering sound in his ear, that mixed in with his dream, a confused vision of long roads and small bright churches, bathed in sun, where birds were perching and singing on high wooden benches and ancient lecterns.

Finally he woke up, noticed, Terence, James's servant, standing by the side of the bed. Geneviève was still sleeping; her regular breathing could be heard in the silence. Christophe signalled the servant to leave and quietly got dressed in the darkness. His teeth rattled: all fires out, the house, the night was freezing. His heart was beating so violently that he had to stop for a moment, and physically grasp it with his hand. He was moved by a feeling of terror and pity. In a low voice, he intoned:

– It's tonight, my God…

Tonight… now perhaps… I have to be there by the bedside, hear his last words, his last breath…

– This old man, whose death I've been waiting for so impatiently, how dear to me he is…he thought.

He left the bedroom and followed the servant, who had remained in the corridor. They crossed the drawing room and went into James's room. He was sitting up in his bed; a coughing fit had just shaken his body: he was trembling like a leaf, trying to catch his breath. A trickle of blood was running down his closed lips.

Christophe, eyes open in involuntary horror, went up to him, drew the old red rep garnet curtains that surrounded the bed, further back. A lamp lit up a pile of untidy papers and James's bare chest, whose emaciated look was frightening. The smell of menthol and ether permeated the room.

Christophe stayed standing in front of him, motionless; James didn't speak; his hands mechanically crumpling his fine silk nightshirt, creasing and smoothing it out over and again, his eyes burning feverishly, deeply hollowed, with a raging fluid blackness, his pallid face, where not a drop of blood seemed to remain. On seeing his son, he pointed to his throat with a feeble movement of his hand.

He gave a vague, grimacing half-smile, in which there was irony, bitterness and perhaps for the first time, a mute appeal for pity, for help; Christophe steeled himself, said to the servant:

– You've telephoned the doctor?

– Yes, monsieur.

Christophe took some small steps toward the bed, held the burning emaciated hand with white nails. But James gently pushed him away:

– No. I'm suffocating!

Christophe went to the chimney place and mechanically warmed his numb hands by the flames.

From this position, turning just a little, he was able to see his father's dying face reflected in the mirror, skeletal, silver-haired, with large feverish eyes. He heard the sound of his strange breathing, short wheezes, that filled the room.

– It's not… the death-rattle…Christophe thought, and his heart seemed to stop beating.

– Of course not, he immediately thought, it's not the moment… Can a man who still speaks, who smiles, be on the point of death?

And, straight away, he felt colder, more tired, felt the light wind blowing through the window. Nearly an hour went by. James stayed motionless, bent in two, breathing in a strange and frightening manner; he brought his handkerchief to his mouth regularly and removed it, each time stained with fresh blood. He lowered his head more and more. Now and again a little sigh of resignation half-opened his lips. Christophe heard the doctor's footsteps, as in a dream. It was four o'clock. He hadn't moved and he felt the cold marble of the fireplace chill his fingers. The doctor asked some questions in a low voice, then he gently wiped James's forehead, covered in sweat, with a thin cloth.

– Be patient, dear monsieur, it's nothing, it'll pass…

He was a small thin man with a lorgnette, his face was ornamented with a black beard. He looked at Bohun with compassion:

– I assure you, dear monsieur, I don't see anything serious. If you like, I could give a small injection to make you more comfortable. Would you like that?

James slowly shrugged his shoulders, exhaled:

– Yes.

– I'm going to boil the water, murmured Christophe.

Passing in front of the doctor, he looked at him questioningly, saw him turn his head and sigh, and understood.

He went into the kitchen where the water was ready on the stove, poured a strong, bitter cup of tea, and swallowed it, burning hot. But he wasn't able to control the slight tremor in his limbs.

He came back into the bedroom, sat down in an armchair near the bed; the doctor yawned and dozed off in his corner.

Both of them jumped, on hearing James's voice:

– There hasn't been anything for a long time, now…

– Papa, murmured Christophe, his voice abruptly filling with tears.

James smiled. Christophe looked at him more closely, astonished, thinking it was an involuntary muscular contraction, but no, it was the old smile he knew so well, weary and mocking.

– Kit…

The old man gestured, as if to touch his son's cheek with his burning fingers. But this ghost of a movement seemed to exhaust him. He let his hand fall, and, straight away, his long fingers began to gently move in the emptiness, began to fold and unfold the sheet in slow repetitive movements. His large feverish eyes fixed upon Christophe, but seemed to search beyond his visible features for a mysterious sign, that only they could decipher. The trickle of dark blood began to run from his half-open lips along his waxen face.

The doctor kept quiet. Only the clock ticking, and the crackling of the fire, could be heard.

Christophe, instinctively lowering his voice, asked:

– Are you in pain?

– No.

– Do you want anything?

– Nothing, murmured the old man, indifferently.

A little later, he allowed himself to be injected by the doctor, with the same unmoving face. He seemed to sleep; only his chest rose, expiring a continuous dull crackle, but his features looked peaceful, at times his mouth trembled, forming a painful little grimace.

Christophe, sitting next to him, remained motionless, head between his hands. All of a sudden a dry sob shook him. He got up and rushed out of the room.

He walked straight ahead, crossing the apartment without looking. Going past the linen-room, he saw Terence, the old man who'd been in James Bohun's service for many years. He was shining a lamp along the shelves of a wardrobe. It was half-empty. He looked for a long time, then finished by pulling out some white pyjamas, which he carefully folded.

Christophe shivered, rapidly pushed open the drawing room door, and found his son in there, sitting next to a gramophone which was playing, surrounded by a pile of cushions; in passing through, he muttered a soft breathless sound, a kind of muffled groan.

Philippe was barefoot in pyjamas, he was holding his unkempt head in his hands and humming, while swaying lightly from side to side.

– Are you mad? Christophe asked dryly.

Philippe stopped the record without responding. He got up; his father said;

– Why the devil are you here?

– I heard a noise, Philippe murmured.

He stretched out his hand, clicked his fingers, and asked nervously:

– Do you have a cigarette?

He took some quick puffs. Christophe saw that his lips were trembling.

– You know that grandpa's dying?

– I know, Philippe said, indifferently.

But his face was pale, and a strange expression hung on in the depths of his eyes. Christophe felt a sudden fondness for him, mixed with compassion. He went up to him. Philippe turned his head, looked at him again with remarkable seriousness.

In a clumsy embarrassing gesture, Christophe pinched his cheek.

– Does it bother you? he asked mechanically.

Philippe shook his head:

– No…

After a moment's reflection he added, and a little grimace of disgust half-twisted his lips:

– To have lived like him, and to finish like this… it's…it's stupid…

– Yes, said Christophe.

– Papa, Philippe began, but immediately stopped.

– He too, Christophe thought, doesn't know how to ask for help…

He asked gently:

– What is it old man?

A dark colour rose into Philippe's cheeks, the painful flush that Christophe knew so well, that slowly invaded his own face when a disarming word tried to penetrate the secrets of his heart.

– He's seeing death for the first time. It's unforgettable. He'll never forget this night...

They meditated in silence, words halted on their lips, held back by a strange kind of inhibition.

All of a sudden Philippe shrugged his shoulders in anger.

– I never loved him. His death means nothing to me.

The ferocious, bitter tone astonished Christophe, accustomed to the cool calmness of his son. Almost immediately, Philippe tried to take it back, concentrated on blowing out smoke, murmured at last, in an ironic way:

– Don't take any notice, papa...I've got personal problems, nothing to do with the earthly end of a great financier. No, I never loved him. A person like him, at least, should never be beaten. But despite everything I'm surprised, sadly surprised, he added, stressing the words, as if he was himself evaluating their banality, their pettiness, and could only pronounce them with self-conscious irony, I'm surprised by this frightening daily event, that I'm seeing for the first time. Death is...

He interrupted himself, looked at his father and said:

– Probably you get used to it as you get older...besides all feelings have to get blunted...

– Death is familiar to me, Christophe said. The war, despite everything, did some good.

He shook with surprise on hearing his son murmur:

– Ah! yes, it's true, you were in the war, you were lucky...

– You're mad, son.

Philippe shook his head:

– No, no, I assure you, I envy you. At least it shakes up the nerves, to think about death isn't a happy thought, but to think about life, life in the present, that's really horrible!

– You're so miserable, my darling? Christophe asked in an undertone, At your age?

– Of course, do you think I'm happy? To have to worry all the time that one'll stay out of work, subordinate one's life to the unhappy obligation of earning one's daily bread?...Does that fill a person with joy? Do you think you can understand me? Your generation was worried, he added laughing: ah! lucky devils!...We others, we aren't worried, we're furious.

– It'll pass, Christophe said in a weary voice.

– You don't understand. You're old, papa.

– You think that a forty-three year old codger only needs a wheel-chair and eventually a shroud, said Christophe, making an effort to laugh. Thanks very much, son.

But Philippe wasn't listening. He sighed, angrily:

– To be eighteen years old, to feel that youth is precious and irreplaceable, and that it's poisoned by worries, by lack of money...it's...it's revolting, it's not fair…It's not my fault, if everything that makes life worth living costs money…

He went silent, began unthinkingly to restart the gramophone.

– No, son, Christophe said, gently… Let him die in peace… He's suffered the same problems as us; he had no more of a sense of wellbeing, of interior peace, than we do. We're all of the same blood…

– Perhaps, Philippe said.

Christophe put out his hand, wanting to stroke his son's hair as he had in the past. But as soon as his fingers touched the brylcreemed surface, he quickly pulled them away, said with a constrained little laugh:

– You've still got a bit of sympathy for your old father, then?

– Of course, Philippe said, feebly.

Christophe lowered his head and went out. He felt as if he'd banged it against a brick wall.

18

A few moments before death, the old man made a beckoning sign with his hand, or at least he forced himself to lift up his hand, his long, thin, transparent fingers. Nobody saw it, nobody except Christophe recognised it. Heart pounding, he got up and approached the bed. James turned his eyes toward him. For the first time, they no longer had their weary mocking expression, and the feverish look had been extinguished. They seemed to be deeply embedded in a waxen mask, on which a glacial sweat was slowly running. A long painful sigh lifted his chest. Christophe leant over him, waited for a moment, as he seemed to see his lips tense with effort, perhaps to form a word?... a call?.. a wish?... But James fell back on his pillow, and immediately a strange and terrifying change appeared on his features. Two deep furrows spread across the white face. The last wheeze had escaped from between his dry breathless lips with the silent sigh he exhaled, a sigh that terminated a long and difficult life, full of vain triumphs and obscure disasters.

James was buried on a winter morning, so mild and sunny that the birds, surprised by the sudden warmth, were singing in the cemetery.

– Why this casket, Christophe thought, this tomb masonry that prevents the earth from eating the bones, transforming them as quickly as possible, into plants, into fertile land?

He noticed a beautiful tree growing nearly at the head of the tomb, and he thought with a hopeful comforting feeling, that the long sinuous roots of the tree would slide very quickly, soon find a way between the stones to absorb the dead body, transform it into leaves, sap, light…

But, abruptly, he saw again in his memory the soft silver hair, that he had stroked for the last time the night before, on the bed, when the old man had expired, and at the thought that he would never again feel that living head under his hand, his heart broke. He feared he was going to weep. He suddenly lowered his face and a light grimace passed across his features.

The ceremony was short; there weren't any friends at James Bohun's obsequies and little interest, he had left the world's stage a long time ago.

The day dragged on. In the evening, Christophe went, as usual, to the little English bar where he drank more than he had done for months.

The Christmas tree hadn't been taken down, but needles were falling all over the place, and the penetrating scent of resin floated in the air. Christophe imagined Norwegian forests, the snow, fir trees, frost… To get away, my God, and on my own!… Alone for ever!… What a dream!… Could it be possible, now?… He looked into the bottom of his glass, full of those cloudy dregs where he found the truth.

– Is it possible that at this point, I'm so taken up with, obsessed by the desire for money, that even this evening, the first evening after my father's death, I can think of that?...

But as soon as he had let the thought of money invade his brain, he was carried away by it; it rose up in his soul and covered him like a flood.

– And if he hasn't left anything?... It's strange, I have the presentiment that he's left nothing... Yet, how has he lived up until today? By what miracle?... But if, however?... The expenses, the doctors, the funeral bills...My God, what a life, what a sordid odious life!... And if there really isn't anything left, I'm imprisoned, press-ganged for the rest of my life... An obscure employee my whole life long, my unique and precious life...

He looked at the men around him with a dismal pity, these anxious, lined faces, these faded eyes. "Everybody lives that way?... But I couldn't give a damn!... I'm quite happy for my housekeeper to waste her life, her unique and precious life, washing tiles to earn her daily bread, but me, me, Christophe Bohun!... Life goes by so quickly, and soon there'll be nothing but a cold, narrow, tomb, and what does it give me, my life?... I get up, I get dressed, I shave, I read and write some idiotic letters, I eat, I sleep... To give up one's life?... Good, but at least for something other than daily bread!... For several years after the war there was the illusion of success, the most brutal and material of successes, but, hey, it had its value!... While now... The generation of the crisis, he thought. My father, he lived differently... If he could see me, how he'd have to smile... once again he saw the sad penetrating smile of old Bohun... Yet he too was gullible, he'd amassed riches which ran away through his fingers, like water... James Bohun, in the past, James Bohun, rich and strong, youthful James Bohun..."

He pulled the dice shaker nervously toward him, began to throw the jacks mechanically in the air, which fell with a light clickety-clack each time in a different way, showing a picture, a different combination every time. He felt tired and drunk; his mind seemed to be divided into two distinct parts; one was passionately interested in the fleeting patterns formed by the moving dice, the other traced a painful memory from the past. James Bohun, young, delicate, pale, fragile, with his cold bright eyes, hair, that he had only ever known white, with streaks of silver... "The Bohun of steel..." His flowers, the fire that he cherished... Yesterday, the servant searching for white pyjamas in the half-empty wardrobe, in which to bury James Bohun. He saw once again, with the painful detail of a dream, the tired servant, yawning, lifting an electric bulb on the end of a long wire to head height, and shining it along the shelves, while James Bohun was fighting for his breath in the room next door. Christophe gritted his teeth with a stifled little groan. That decline, those years of suffering and immobility...That solitude, and before... that vain labour... He rattled the dice for a long time in his closed hands. He fixed his eyes on the mirror above the bar which reflected his own image. His son, he thought, what buffoonery... No, I wouldn't have wanted the life he loved so much... He fought against money, in the beginning, when he was young and strong, he triumphed over it…In the end, he was brought down by it…

– He interrupted himself, thinking angrily:

– What idiotic ideas…

But, in spite of himself, he saw this life as a hard battle.

Perhaps he found it amusing at the beginning… But at the end?...

No, no, not for anything in the world, a departure like his, he murmured. I'm not one of his race!... I want to be delivered from the tyranny of money, and from the hateful work that procures it… I hate that. I want… but, so much for my wants, there isn't a name… in any language… and yet, it's an obscure desire, unformulated, in all of us who are here, nine tenths of the world… It's strange… An avalanche of gold, he thought, that my father and his like, set in motion, which crushed them, which continues to slide, and is crushing me in my turn, me… How tired I am…

Again, he slowly rattled the dice, looked fixedly into the mirror, which became obscured under some thick, dark smoke. He had a strange sensation of losing himself, of being split in two. The negro was just coming in. He stared as if he had difficulty recognising him, the pale brownish-yellow face, his white crew-cut hair, his short snowy moustache, the gold tooth that appeared in each angle of his mouth in a sad sardonic smile. Christophe signalled him to come over.

– *Yea, Sir?*

– Play, old man…

With a movement of his lips, he gently indicated his preferred tune.

The negro played a short intro.

–*Yea, Sir?*

–Yes, said Christophe.

The negro began to play; Christophe put his head in his hands and listened to the guitar weeping and whining, and the old nasal voice, until morning.

– Love? he thought abruptly, with a kind of despair, a vain cry for help, Love?... Murielle?... No!... To hell with love!... Scarcely still good for Philippe... For me?... To hell, he repeated, savagely.

No more money in the bank
No cute baby we can spank
Oh what to do? Oh, what to do?
Put out the lights and go to bed.

19

The next day, Geneviève and Christophe were alone in the apartment, where the strange smell of phenol and faded flowers that remains after a death, still lingered. Geneviève murmured:

– My love, we need to go through your father's papers, destroy what's useless…It'll take your mind off your grief… Anyway, perhaps there's a will…

– I understand, Christophe said softly.

Oh, what to do? Oh, what to do? He held back a sad little sardonic smile with difficulty. Poor Geneviève… her soul was full of scruples, decency… "My poor Geneviève…"

He entered James Bohun's bedroom behind her, turned around frowning, covering up his feelings with a nervous grin, the empty bed, so flat, so small, covered with a white sheet. The fire was out in the fireplace, the ashes carefully brushed. Old Bohun was irremediably absent.

– I'll leave you, murmured Geneviève.

He took several steps, stopped in front of the closed desk, touched the drawers one by one, hesitatingly; finally he sat down in his father's armchair, the old armchair in red rep fabric, slid his hand gently over the little bronze lion's head that ornamented the arms. He remained still for a long time, looking at the desk without opening it. A will… That's a real Geneviève idea, a Geneviève Courtenay one… A will, that presupposes that one cares, more or less, what's going to happen to those who come after yourself…

– He did love me, he thought, the way he loved all things, scornfully... Yet the words, "love", "to love", fitted so badly with what he knew of James.

– And I, do I love my son, my wife, my mistress, the way a normal man does?... I?... The same blood... he said out loud.

He pulled the first drawer towards him, empty; only an old cheque book with torn out cheques, whose remaining stubs fell into his hands. Further back, some letters... an unknown hand, dating back fifteen or twenty years... the signature of a woman on a card...a yellowed photograph, a woman's face, surmounted by a large hat ornamented with feathers, and covered by a white veil. Below, some indecipherable words. His own letters to his father, dated on the front. He raised his eyebrows. That seemed so little like James, that... sentimentality... But, perhaps, he had the neurosis common to some men, of automatically keeping all the papers he received, even down to the most insignificant...

– I'll never know anything, he thought. And moreover, that's the way of things. It'll be the same when I'm dead, Philippe will open my drawers, find well organised photos of himself, his childhood letters, those he wrote to me at the age of five: " Papa, I really love you..." Like me, he'll shrug his shoulders, and think: " Old age madness... As he certainly never loved me..."

Some other pale, torn snaps were lying around in the corners, his mother, unknown women... "That's not, that's not what I want to see... Some memories from his own childhood, his parents, when they were young..." But he didn't find anything.

Not an object, not a story, just the name of an obscure Greek village. Nothing. He didn't have anyone in the world, so alone, so detached from everything... My family?... Family, what an incomprehensible word...

Finally, his hand encountered an old black leather wallet; he opened it; the frayed silk tore under his fingers; three one-thousand-franc notes remained folded in the inside pocket, and a cheque for ten thousand francs, which had not yet been cashed, and which bore the signature of Beryl. On seeing it, Christophe shook with surprise. A letter was attached to the cheque, a short note consisting of these words:

" Please find a cheque for ten thousand francs enclosed, the end of December payment, as agreed."

Christophe slammed the drawer closed

– I don't understand, he said aloud. Am I dreaming? He's been getting money from Beryl?... Settlements for old accounts, perhaps?... But no, no, there must be something else...

He opened some other drawers. Empty, empty. Only the last contained an envelope, placed in an obvious position, bearing the address in pencil on the outside, written in his father's trembling hand:

For Christophe,

Gently, controlling the shaking of his hands, he tore it open. To his inexplicable surprise, a wad of old, yellow press-cuttings fell out, memos from the Beryl Agency during the period 1924-1925, together with a letter addressed to James Bohun. He read:

"… So long as the cabinet doesn't change its mind, there is no chance, despite our joint efforts, of bringing about a war, or, what would amount to the same thing for us, hostile preparations by a warmongering government or country. I count on your influence without which we won't get anywhere. See attached, the list of names requested, with the account of sums received.

" Beryl"

Christophe rapidly scanned the names, on a loose sheet pinned to the page. All the names of compromised parliamentarians, journalists and financiers, were marked with dates and sums received. A total of twenty.

At the bottom of the sheet, in pencil, the same trembling hand of the old man had written:

Your inheritance, Kit.

Christophe threw his head back abruptly, knocking his fist against the cold little mouth that embellished the arm of the chair, and began to laugh nervously. On hearing Geneviève's footsteps in the corridor, he stopped himself and quietly closed the dossier. The sun had moved around; it lit up the empty bed.

20

Christophe irritably crumpled up the letter and the list that he had just re-read. He was sitting at his desk in Beryl's. It was his slackest hour at the end of the day. In a neighbouring room, someone was continually shouting: " Allo! Allo! Clermont-Ferrand !..." The building resonated with the sound of footsteps, voices, doors being closed, the clickety-clack of typewriters, the regular screeching of their carriages that slid along under the hand of the typists with a monotonous, sharp little cry. Some faint ringing sounds came from the director's office. Outside, the rain was falling. Christophe shivered nervously, and his face twisted into a harsh grimace, so strange that the employee on the neighbouring table, looked up and stared. He was a blond young man called Ludovic Pêche. He sorted out the post that had to be taken to Beryl for signing every evening. The radiators were overheating, giving off an odour of paint and glue. Six o'clock sounded.

Christophe got up and went to the window. He watched the wet roofs for a long time, the sky, where a feeble silver light shone between two clouds.

– Allo! Allo! Clermont-Ferrand! the weary voice repeated behind the wall.

– I'm tired, thought Christophe, feeling overwhelmed, three nights without sleep and those awful last days…

He sighed, mentally repeated:

– Let's see, we have to think of… to think of…

His mind seemed to turn, lazily, in a sort of mysterious circle, and to come up against an invisible object every time. The image of James's empty bedroom kept returning in his memory, and that of the small, chequered, green leather cushion, that he had slid beneath the head of the dead man.

– Father?... Yes, he murmured impatiently, but he's dead, he's at peace now... But me?... I have to pull myself together... God! How annoying... What a stupid story, he murmured with a near physical sense of disgust: Father?... He would have set fire to Europe with those papers, and my youth... But me? Me? To lump me together with people like Beryl, to own newspapers and topple ministries. That doesn't appeal, he thought, with a kind of ironic despair, and the worst is that nothing appeals to me, neither that, nor... the other thing... As evidently there is still a way... One could handle this "inheritance" another way... A campaign against the steel merchants, the capitalists, society, don't I know?... I couldn't give a damn. Let them die!... I want some peace! Money?...

– He was right, my lad... It's not our fault... But money, the instrument of power, money, the instrument of hate and domination!... What a joke, what an enormous joke!... I want leisure, laziness, tranquillity, to neither vegetate nor fight against myself, but to live!... Is that so impossible?... Why wasn't I born into my wife's family? A landed gentleman, but they no longer exist... To think that people in the past complained, my God... To live in an undisturbed garden, somewhere in Amboise or

Châteauroux, to have never known and never desired anything else!... what a dream...

He began to slowly turn around in the room, half-whistling between his closed lips.

"Beryl..."

He felt an uncontrollable need to see Beryl; in spite of himself he waited for the telephone to ring, which had summoned his neighbour into the director's office.

A feeling of curiosity, cruelty, a very light frisson of pleasure disturbed him, and he enjoyed it, like the rare moments when Murielle's voice awoke desire.

He said abruptly:

– Would you let me take the boss's mail in your place, old man? You'd be doing me a kindness.

– If you like, said the surprised youngster.

Christophe took the packet of letters that he handed him, but an ironic detachment invaded him once again; he shrugged his shoulders, thinking:

– We'll see.

Just at that moment the telephone rang; he heard the echo of Beryl's voice groaning:

– Mail.

He silently followed the long corridor and went into Beryl's room. The directorial office was dark and immense; a large map of Europe ornamented one of the walls. A metal lamp on the table, its stem pulled down, lit Beryl's lowered head. He had unfastened his collar and was breathing heavily; his double chin was compressed against his chest and the heat produced fine drops of sweat that made the soft sagging flesh on his face and cheeks shine. "A collapsed pudding", Christophe thought with dark humour.

However, he raised his eyebrows in surprise when Christophe came in, immediately pulling himself together. He indicated a chair with a sullen gesture and held out his hand to take the mail. He began to cast his eye over the letters and sign them.

Christophe waited.

– Pen, grumbled Beryl.

Christophe passed his own across. Beryl looked up and said with a forced laugh, as if he'd seen him for the first time.

– Ah! ah! so it's you, young man?... I didn't recognise you. We don't often have the pleasure of seeing you in the office these days.

– No, Christophe said softly.

– Sick?

– Mourning, Christophe said, indicating his black armband, didn't you know?

Beryl fell back in his chair, and said with an effort, in a changed voice:

– No, I didn't know... Your father?... But how come that I didn't know anything? I would have considered it a duty to be at the funeral; I'm honoured to have been one of your father's oldest colleagues. There wasn't an announcement in the papers was there?

– Just family, Christophe said.

– Ah yes...

Christophe thought:

– There are two ways. To continue the blackmail. Why be frightened of words?... Or play the big game. Act as my father would have done in my place. Out him, fight him, etc., etc., etc. God, how dramatic this makes me seem, childish... Yet, will it be so easy to fight, the old fox?... My father was a redoubtable adversary. Old, sick, but cut out of the same material, still the same race. Me? I'm not strong. Even if he folds, he'll come back quickly, he'll get me off his back one way or another. In order to get the better of a man like Beryl, you have to be a James Bohun, or have a lot of money behind you. But above all you have to love life, this precious existence. The power of these people is that in defending their money, they defend their life itself. And they know how to hate, take revenge, all sorts of primitive feelings, for me, at least... In this instance, I harbour a certain pleasure in holding back, making him sweat by my silence. He's waiting, he's lowering his nose, he's stiffening his back, is he preparing a trick, to shut me up, or to fight? He's thinking, he's examining me, he's sizing me up... Well no, no, decidedly, that no longer excites me, he thought, ironically, bluff itself no longer excites me. I don't even enjoy it in a poker game, my word... And to get an income from that? No!

An abrupt flush mounted to his cheeks.

– It's pride, stupid pride. It's only pride. But it's stronger than me! Simple blackmail that would be so easy, I can't do it!

With an effort of will he calmed himself, thought ironically:

– Yet, how much would he give me? How much would be sufficient to live from now on, as I wish, to support those who depend on me?... Millions?

Nowadays, "dishonour" isn't worth so much! And for a lesser sum, it's really not worth it!... No, what has its charm, its value, is to do what my father did in his youth, to topple him, to take his place, to make him serve me… and others!

He slowly shrugged his shoulders. However, Beryl pushed the pile of signed letters towards him.

They looked at each other for a moment.

Christophe abruptly thought:

– But, but… isn't he going to make the first move and kick me out? My God, that's what I'd do in his place!... Ah! no, no, me, James Bohun's son, to feel like a sucker and… No! I have to do it in my father's memory… Wait a bit, old man…

– You knew my father well in your youth, when you started up, no? he said through clenched teeth.

They slowly sized each other up. Beryl inclined his head.

– Yes, he eventually said. He was a man…

He stopped, searching for his words, and doubtless, made a decision.

– A very powerful man.

– Nothing's going to change in my position in this business, Christophe asked after a silence, as a result of this death?

He watched Beryl curiously. He was waiting for a refusal, a sign of trouble, he waited for them, perhaps even hoped for them. But Beryl was quiet. He played absent-mindedly with the electric light switch for a moment, putting it on and off jerkily. Finally, he sighed, looked up at Christophe and said, emphasising the last couple of words:

– Nothing, monsieur Bohun.

21

The same night in the marital bed, lying motionless next to Geneviève, Christophe recounted the events of the day.

He was lying on his back, arms crossed behind his head; he spoke slowly in a monotonous ironic voice.

Geneviève listened to him without saying a word.

He felt for a cigarette on the bedside table, lit it, slowly inhaled the smoke. Finally he asked with a nervous little laugh:

– You understand me?

– Yes, she said with a gentle sigh, and… Was that all?... There wasn't anything else in your father's desk?

Absolutely nothing, my dear.

He burst out laughing in spite of himself; she shook nervously, asked:

– But what's this Christophe?

– It's funny, he said.

He stretched out his hand in the dark, searched for hers, took it:

So? I've done well to have no truck with this last paternal gift?

But, how could you have done otherwise? she said… That would have been vile.

– Madame de Fleurville, he thought smiling, with a feeling of sad irony, that's the only argument that didn't come to mind. In the end I acted as he would have done, and our wellbeing's safe.

He couldn't stop himself murmuring softly:

– Isn't that so, my darling?... I knew you'd share my view...

He heard her sigh lightly:

– Christophe...

– Yes?

She moved nearer him, stoked his face softly in the dark with her hand.

– Christophe, my love, money doesn't buy happiness.

– Of course, of course...

– You have your own conscience.

– Certainly, he murmured in a weary voice. And don't forget the esteem of honest men...

He took her warm hand that was caressing his cheek and lowered it with a mocking tenderness:

– We'll have to sell the furniture, she said in an undertone.

– Yes. And the car.

– A little three-roomed apartment, she finished dreamily. But we could be happy there, happier than now.

Christophe put his cheek in her hand, looked fixedly into the darkness; on the writing desk facing the bed, a small silver vase was shining alone in the shadows; a distant ray from a car's headlamp crossed the room; rain fell on the windowsill.

– There you are, Christophe thought. A full stop. A finished chapter. What now? Leave the apartment? Sell the furniture? Doubtless, about fifty for the funeral expenses, the doctor's bill, death duties, and then, my God, we only have to live, to keep on going. Happier than now, Geneviève says, that's a delicious irony... in short, she's right. For eight years my life has been just the same as it will go on being from now on, but without the bright spots that make it tolerable. At least there's nothing more to hope for. What peace, he said in an undertone.

But Geneviève didn't hear.

– What does she think about? She doesn't seem unhappy. I wouldn't swear that an obscure satisfaction isn't beginning to show through her disappointment. A sunny little apartment, me, always there, at hand, and for good reason! A housemaid that she could boss around, train up… She'll cook me nice little meals. I won't miss out on anything. Everything will be nice and tidy, polished furniture, the smell of caustic soda and stews will fill the place. Why do I pity myself? The ideal, the dream, he murmured, burying a savage little snigger in the pillow.

Geneviève started:

– Aren't you asleep yet, Christophe?...You seem agitated?

– Not at all, I assure you.

– It's late. We should sleep.

She hesitated for a moment and said in a different voice:

– It's a sad thing too, for Murielle.

– Why?

– But… because… won't she have to go back to live with her husband?... We won't have the necessary means…

– Yes, yes, he said abruptly, I understand. Well, she'll go, what do you want me to do?

He interrupted himself, as his voice faded away. Murielle… So nothing of the past would remain?… He would enter, living, into a gloomy tomb, a dark empty sepulchre, where he would only have to stay quietly imprisoned, and wait for death.

He trembled painfully, interrogated his heart:

– Do I still love her?

He mused:

– No. I only cry for myself.

22

The apartment Geneviève found, occupied the top floor of a building in Passy, dating from 1900, the only one in Paris still decorated with pink curlicues and stained-glass windows. Clothes shops, Prisunics, stocking sellers under the portes cochères, boutiques offering haberdashery, groceries, pink mannequins on display in a hairdressers, and a little open air market, populated the street outside. Huge painted cardboard giants guarded the façade of a cinema on the corner of the neighbouring avenue. The house had a respectable middle class appearance. The staircase was narrow, the treads were covered in grey twill with red borders; the lift had the form of action and spacial capacity of an egg dancing on a jet of water; the apartment consisted of three small rooms, cheap and cheerful, the stained-glass window in the bathroom was rose and green; the radiators were white hot, the walls freshly redecorated, giving off a smell of paint.

When Christophe first saw it, he'd laughed and agreed to everything: a nervous cheerfulness animated him.

One evening, one of the last they spent together in avenue Marceau, Murielle said to him in an undertone:

– My word, you seem happy.

– My despondency exceeds my hopes, he said smiling.

They were alone in the living room, around the small coke fire.

Even these red embers, Christophe looked at them lovingly...In the neighbouring room, Geneviève was sorting out the drawers; she crossed the living room carrying piles of linen in her arms. She had lost weight, a wrinkle was beginning to form on her face which hadn't previously been there, which made her cheek more sculpted and hollow.

They heard her footsteps get further away. Christophe became sad again, twisted and broke in two the matches he was mechanically taking out of the box and spreading out on the arms of the chair. Still other things were weighing on his conscience... this silent woman, who was leaving, whom he would no longer see, who was waiting for some words, some caresses...

– Lover and mistress, after all, he thought in a kind of stupor. But what could he say? Geneviève, at least, was quiet, and resigned, I've had enough of these women, he thought angrily.

She leaned forward. She scrutinised his face avidly, in the light of the fire.

– Christophe, I'm leaving soon.

He didn't know how to reply, and she turned away silently. They heard Geneviève's footsteps in the adjoining room.

He took Murielle's hand in the darkness, twisted nervously, cruelly, her abandoned fingers.

– I want to spend a day alone with you, she said painfully, through clenched teeth.

– It's difficult, Christophe murmured, uneasily.

– I've never asked you for anything.

He hesitated:

– Well the car hasn't been sold yet. We're leaving together on Sunday. But Geneviève...

– Geneviève won't be coming.

– Ah, that's what you think?

– I'm sure of it.

He shrugged his shoulders:

– OK, he murmured lazily. If you like...

23

Springtime had come, sharp, impatient, anxious. The march wind was violently shaking the young leaves, half-desiccated and once again curled by the cold nights; it passed under the chimney flue-shutters and whistled like a fife. But the air was softer, purer; the first lilacs were decorating the pony-traps.

They had to move by the 15th April, and Murielle to leave for Rome.

Life, stretched out in front of Christophe, long and monotonous. So long and so depressing did it seem, that he forced himself to close his eyes and not think of the future, beyond each short day bounded by sleep. Even so, from time to time, the despair at the bottom of his soul was awakened and gripped him with a deep, dull, ache, gnawed at him like a wound. Every living being looks for happiness; there wouldn't be any more for him on this earth. To work, to slave away incessantly, without hope! Only the rent, taxes, gas and electricity bills, marked out his life with their sordid unbearable deadlines!

– Millions of people exist and are happy with this life!... No!... No!... It's a lie, he thought passionately: they resign themselves because they're ashamed to admit being preoccupied with the *material side* of existence. Shame?... What a great joke!... Give us something else…

In April, the real spring, warm, blazing and radiant, abruptly penetrated the smoke, the petrol fumes, the noise and bad smells of Paris; it filled the air with light and flame; for two weeks, it intoxicated people, still adjusted and resigned to the blackness of winter, and it passed like a storm.

One morning, Christophe and Murielle went out. It was a Sunday; they had left the house early enough, at seven o'clock; the roads were still empty.

They were going for lunch at an inn near Chartres. The white building was surrounded by a long narrow garden, where more vegetables than flowers were growing. In places between the beds, April was still showing, a pink bare earth.

A bucket was being drawn from a well with the creaking sound of a turning pulley; it rose slowly into the sun, full of dark limpid water. The deep silence relaxed their overwrought nerves, calmed their tired hearts; their eyes themselves felt soothed by the softness of the undulating country and the grey, slightly stormy horizon, the way it happens on the most beautiful days, when one turns toward Paris.

Right from the start, a strange joy, strong and hot, took hold of them. It brought back the past, the country-drives in an open-topped car, the crazy nights spent... They became silent: What good talking? They each knew exactly what scenes were being revived in the other's memory, guessing the words, words of love, that weren't being said by lips unused to kissing.

– Perhaps I'm only regretting my youth? Christophe thought with a stubborn hope: perhaps... But I'm not old. Forty-three, it's young... Murielle, she's my past... But there were plenty of other women like her, other beautiful twenty-year-old girls, who touched my heart, got my blood boiling, in the past…

He sighed:

– The beautiful sun… the spring, the suns of the past… Finished, finished for ever… But it was beautiful then, he thought, that memory of the past, a short stormy past, which had retained all its flavour, its first flowering, never to be sullied by words, inconvenient memories that had lain intact through so many years, at the bottom of their hearts.

At that moment, with the first soft April sun warming their leaning shoulders, with that deep peaceful sky above their heads, the feeling that the whole of life was at an end, that all joy had fled, scarcely saddened them. They were quiet, remembering. Making eye-contact with one another, just occasionally, with effort, as in the past. But Christophe turned away from his memories: he remembered Murielle's eyelids only too well, which he had so often kissed, curved like shells, with a delicate bluish ring surrounding them, rekindling again their fragile flowery colour. Eyelids, now blackened, crumpled, swollen at the edges, and these sad, weary eyes, where languor and desire burned, despite the years, like a dark flame.

It was nearly two o'clock. They had lost their way. They had followed a deserted road for some time, between two rows of fruit trees that the unaccustomed heat had covered with white blossom during the night. At that moment, a gentle grey sky illuminated the trees and the delicate still blossoms from afar, as if with light rays from a reflector placed low on the horizon.

The sky was radiant now, deep blue, and one could hear birds on the branches singing joyfully.

There weren't many people about, just some couples, lingering in the arbours, but the rest had already eaten and drunk their fill, and the cars had gone.

Christophe pursed his lips, breathed in the air; in spite of the sun and the heat, the taste was sharp and cold, a little bitter; he remembered that winter had. scarcely passed.

– I'm hungry, Murielle said.

She laughed, as in past times. As in times past, he tried to get sight of the reflection of her teeth, that pale flash which glimmered, every now and then, between her painted lips. What a beautiful mouth she still had... it had lost the pure, proud bow whose memory he treasured, but it was beautiful, still...

He looked at her for a long time, penetrating her eyes with his gaze. She took his hand. A frisson of passion went through his body again. He savoured this flux and reflux of love, which ebbed and flowed in them like the sea's tides, in a strange and bitter way.

He thought abruptly:

– After all, what does it matter?... One never has the life one wants. That he's staying with Geneviève, that she's returning to her husband. What can that stop from happening?... She'll come to Paris. Pena, hadn't he met him in Paris in the autumn? And if it's there, love, desire, the rest, one can get over, doesn't mean a thing, the rest is nothing.

He laughed:

– Me too, I'm dying of hunger!

They went to eat. The restaurant was renowned for its fine food and good wines. At first they ate and drank joyfully. Then, Murielle, was the first to become silent. Christophe continued to drink. Imperceptibly his mood changed; a black irritability invaded him once again. Our day's running out, and tomorrow... what's left to expect? Life in the little apartment in Passy... Lord, the pink curlicues, the egg-yellow basements...clean and tidy, full to the brim with Geneviève's presence. What more?... To sell the car. A wave of suffering went through him. Probably no holidays, neither this year nor the following, less than two weeks spent in a cheap little hole, in a dozen years not a day of affordable pleasure... " I'll never see the mountains of Engadine, nor the hills of Florence... No! No! Don't think about them anymore! Let's forget! Let's forget! I was nearly happy just now. I was intoxicated..."

Because, in the end, what could a man do? A little leisure, to forget the daily worries for a couple of hours, and feel the spring wind blow back and forth across his face, across the lifted windscreen, and burn his cheeks and face. "Youth is nothing else than perpetual intoxication..." To revive the divine frisson, he poured some wine, the end, but this wasn't it!... He couldn't retrieve the joy which had fled, which had run from him, imperceptibly, the way blood escapes from cut veins in a bath.

Little by little a kind of soothing sadness grew in him. He was eating and feeling pleasure. He said out loud:

– Food and wine are worth more than love.

Murielle had stretched out her hand toward him. He had distinctly seen the light trembling of her fingers, their appealing movement, immediately suppressed. They had fallen under his withering gaze. She turned her eyes away, contemplated the empty garden with an exhausted air.

He drank some more. His head was painful and his heart was heavy, but full of a sad peace. He was no longer looking for lost joy, only this weighty equilibrium that the wine procured, which was necessary for him. He stopped talking. An involuntary expression of sardonic cruelty, of wickedness and mockery passed over his features.

– Why? she thought, brokenheartedly.

For a moment she had the desire to speak to him, to seduce him, but she contented herself with an indifferent shrug of the shoulders.

– Doubtless I'm too old? she thought with bitter resignation.

And similarly he was thinking:

– Perhaps it's simply because she's aged? Of course not, that'd be too easy, and if it wasn't her, it would only be someone else, as I was thinking a moment ago... Was it just now? Or a century ago?... Of course not. It's all over for me, love. At least there was some nobility in my life, Murielle, the shadow, the memory, the ghost of Murielle, brought with it my first and my last love.

Sadly tasting the form of the words on his lips, he said out loud:

– Love…

Eyes lowered, she said softly:

– What?

– Nothing, he muttered cruelly, I was thinking of the past.

– It's only today that everything ended, she murmured, and her husky monotone evoked a storm of memories, regrets, desires in Christophe's heart, lifted it, but it immediately descended into gloomy indifference.

– What's the good?

The air was colder; winter seemed to have returned. The sun went down.

It was late. The wind blew. Murielle, shivering, pulled the top of her woollen coat tightly round her neck.

The first, she murmured:

– It's late.

– Yes.

He stubbed out his cigarette ponderously on the side of his saucer. Later, and at the moment of death, he would see that blue saucer, and the first wasp, still active, which was greedily sucking some half-dissolved sugar from a drop of coffee that had run down the cup.

Darkness was coming strangely fast, and with it, a sharp biting wind bringing black clouds from the west.

– The weather's changing.

One of them pronounced this phrase in a gloomy voice.

The other said:

Night's going to fall. I hope the headlamps are working properly.

– What's wrong with them? Are they broken?

– The left one's not working properly. I had it repaired, but the mechanic in the little garage doesn't know very much. Anyhow, when I sell the car...

– How much will you sell it for?

– Oh! I don't know, scarcely five thousand francs, it's done a lot of miles...

She sighed softly, a deep sigh exhaled with care, out of keeping with her words:

– Pity...

He took her arms, and with an automatic movement, held her close to him for an instant, experiencing at the same time, with sardonic melancholy, the deep indifference that her body evoked, now that the smoke, the wine, and the sun's springtime heat were dissipated. She was quite right... Only, today, after so many years, the end had come, the story's over... " My life itself is going to end? And it'll begin like this?... Of course not, he replied slowly to himself. It's only youth that's finished. It ends early these days. True youth, that nourishes love. No not love, little sensual encounters, beddings, more or less passionate... But what's left, is the only thing that matters..."

He pulled away from her; his arms fell heavily to the side of his body. They climbed back into the car and left; night had already fallen, and the cold returned freezing her to the bone. She sat sadly and silently, just like himself, buried in old memories.

Life had killed desire, passion, love…There was nothing left.

24

The following Monday, Christophe accompanied Murielle to the train for Rome; they parted silently; he pressed his lips one last time against the cold cheek that she offered him, that she hadn't made up, that suddenly seemed old and worn. She got into the carriage; he saw her walk down the corridor, and disappear; in a moment she approached the window again. The night was all-embracing; a train behind them left, piercing the air with its high-pitched whistle. He could vaguely see the form of her pale face pressed against the window, she shouted some words that he couldn't make out. The train began to move; he took several steps along the platform. She saw that he hadn't heard her words. Nervously, with trembling hands, she lowered the window, leaned out. A platform lantern lit up her pale features, covered in tears. She shouted: "Christophe!" He heard his name, but the rest got lost in the thunderous noise, as the train passed under a glass roof and a vibrating bridge. A thick plume of smoke went up, forming large black clouds, which veiled Murielle's face and completely obscured her, slowly dispersing in the air. Christophe stopped himself. His heart was beating violently. When the smoke had gone and he looked up, the train had departed. He could no longer see the two rails feebly shining in the night. His legs were trembling. He walked slowly toward the station buffet, ordered a coffee, a brandy, drank them standing up, tried to master the fine nervous tremor in his fingers, and his body.

– It's over, my God, too bad, he thought, it's all over… to hell with it now!...

He went back.

When he got home, he saw Geneviève, standing on a ladder, passing a paint-brush across the vestibule's enamelled walls. The smell of turpentine and paint filled the little apartment.

Geneviève was singing to herself; he stopped for a moment, and looked at her with a feeling bordering on hate; the aging face, lifted toward the ceiling, was lit up with a flame of happiness.

On seeing him she asked:

– Has she gone?

– Yes, he said dryly.

She sighed softly, lowered her eyelids, murmured with sincere melancholy and hypocritical pity:

– Poor soul…

He left her, went into the bedroom to lie down, closed the shutters, lay immobile for a long time, breathing the mild perfumed wind that came from the small nearby garden; it was surrounded by a high wall, which covered the trees up to their tops, but, at night-time, puffs of scented vegetation escaped into the air.

Geneviève had followed him into the bedroom; she went up and lay on her elbows at his side. They looked silently out on the dark road, and the buses grinding their way down, scything the night with the long red lights fixed to their sides.

– She imagines she understands me, Christophe thought angrily.

But when she put her hand on his sunken shoulder, the familiar contact with her bare hand brought tears to his eyes. He abruptly moved away.

– Good evening, he murmured between his teeth, and he left the bedroom, the house, and wandered aimlessly half the night, without thinking, along the deserted streets, to the banks of the Seine.

25

Springtime passed. May brought cold weather, scattered showers and abrupt storms; the days grew longer and seemed emptier and more useless than in the heart of winter. Only in June, did the warmth return. But Christophe felt overcome by a strange numbness; he was eating, drinking, sleeping, without thoughts, without desires. He forgot that outside the noise and dust of Paris, the beaches were gilded under the sun and showers, that the sea was blue, striped with gold and flames. Sometimes in the evenings he went alone to a street café bounded by two laurels in containers, aimlessly watched the fountains in the square, under a clear sky, until he felt sleep taking him over. He returned home, lay down and slept soundly until morning.

The weather became hotter. Soon, Philippe left: the cinema company that employed him was shooting in Bandol. From there, he sent a telegram, and eight days later a strange letter where only the post script: I'm no longer drunk, was legible. Then, the correspondence ceased, to be replaced by brief postcards sent from week to week. He wouldn't be coming back to Paris till autumn.

Christophe saw his son's departure with relief. In their large old apartment, his untidiness and general habits were already irritating.

– But here, with cigarette butts in the bath, records spread all over the floor, pictures of his friends, love-letters between the pages of books, it was beginning to seem like a catastrophe, he thought.

Summer... The office at Beryl's where Christophe worked, was situated just below roof level; the walls were painted white; one side was formed by a glazed bay, across which a strip of dazzling light ran; it seemed to go through his eyes and lodge itself inside his skull.

One July evening, Christophe returned home earlier than usual. Geneviève was holding a letter in her hand and conspicuously scanning it with her eyes, doubtless waiting for him to ask what it was, but, barring rare moments, he no longer looked at her familiar face; he said nothing.

The table was laid in front of the open window, through which all the sounds of the street came in. Similarly in the neighbouring houses, every window was open wide, in order to capture the small amount of breathable air that descended from heaven to earth towards evening.

A man in shirt-sleeves was leaning on every window; one could see beds made up for the night, cleared tables; the sound of gramophones, wirelesses, even the distant ringing of telephones, resonated across the narrow street, from house to house, the voices of caretakers seated on the doorsteps, the thunder of lorries running down the carriageway, the laughs and cries of the children, the fracas of their roller skates; the darkening sky; someone in a neighbouring house was playing the violin. Every now and then, out of the droning racket of the road, Christophe noticed some lighter notes escaping, he raised his head and listened silently. From the freshly watered next door garden, some whiffs of perfume rose up and reached him.

One by one the gramophones and wireless sets went off; the violin alone continued playing; a passionate melancholic music passed gently through the blazing air.

– He plays marvellously well, Christophe said, leaning forward in order to see the silhouette holding his violin, but the apartment was dark; only a lamp under a red shade, shone feebly in a corner.

Then someone started the gramophone up again. For a moment the violin fought; one could hear its long breathy phrases resonating, like complaints, like desperate cries; then the window closed. The gramophone alone unwound at its ease in the peaceful evening air:

Elle avait un tout petit menton
Valentine, Valentine
Elle avait de tout petits tétons
Que je tâtais à tâtons[1]

– Darling, Geneviève said, I got a letter from my sister.

– Oh yes, Christophe replied automatically.

– She's invited me to spend a fortnight with them at Courtenay.

Christophe felt an extraordinary sense of contentment; he went up to his wife and abruptly squeezed her hand.

---

[1] She had a pretty little chin
Valentine, Valentine,
She had little tits as well,
That I fondled with my fingers

– But what a good idea, darling!... You can relax, breathe in the country air... After this infernal winter...

She looked down, remained immobile for an instant, played distractedly with her knife.

– I don't want to leave you, Christophe, but we have to say something to my sister...

– What? he murmured, frowning.

– But, love, just think... We wouldn't be able to do it on your three thousand franc salary. You haven't taken account.

He paled, a grimace rapidly twisted his lips.

She continued precipitately:

– An advance, a simple advance, naturally.

– Oh! he said, laughing bitterly, if you're counting on the future, it's my turn to tell you "You haven't taken account..." At Beryl all paths are closed to me. It's impossible to find any other employment at the present time... You aren't unaware that there's a dreadful economic state called a crisis. Perhaps another man could fight it within himself, fight, and win... Not me. Don't have any illusions. I'm too lazy, too egotistical, and I'm not fond enough of life. Don't expect anything from me.

– All the more reason, she said in a low voice.

He smiled with effort:

– That's true.

– I thought, she continued, that my sister and I should have an equal share of Henri's estate.

– Henri?

– Don't you remember? she said reproachfully: is it possible? My older brother, who lives in

Australia. I've often spoken of him. He's rich and childless. I thought, she continued after a moment's silence, that I could commit myself in your name and that of Philippe, to renounce the inheritance in favour of my sister. In exchange, they would give us a small income over several years. Oh!... a thousand francs a month, that's all that I could get... I remember, when I was a child, my father and my uncle Auguste had a similar arrangement.

– My God, but how old is your brother?

– Nearly fifty.

– Is he ill?

– Of course not, I don't think so.

– And you think that your family will dispense a thousand francs a month in the hope of this distant inheritance?

– Distant, of course, she said quickly. You don't know our family spirit, darling, she continued with that superior nuance in her voice and look which appeared whenever she spoke of hers and of Courtenay. My sister has three children, she's wise and forward thinking. If I were in her position, she continued, sighing, I'd do the same thing. It's by foresight and economy that the fortunes of our province were founded, she added, repeating words she'd heard in her childhood, which escaped from her lips, no doubt dictated by a line of dead, wise burgers of Courtenay, sleeping in the peace of the Lord.

He shrugged his shoulders in a familiar gesture:

– You're right , my darling.

She was dreaming, her eyes lost in the distance.

– Four thousand francs per month… With four thousand francs per month we could live well enough. Luckily, the apartment is a bargain. We won't have to complain, she said.

He got up, leaned across her, half closed his eyes. Very far, behind the closed windows, the voice of the violin could be heard again.

Intoxicated, he listened for a long time.

– But what is it? Whatever is it?

He said out loud:

– Ah! yes… The Magic Flute… *Zauberflöte*…

He thought with a strange despair:

– I can't even hear the music…it's breaking my heart…

26

Christophe remained sitting on the window sill for half the night; sometimes he leaned outside mechanically, to try and catch a breath of fresher air. But as the night went on, it became overwhelmingly hot and dry. Only the smell of petrol came up from the road and a burning grit that crackled between his teeth.

– That's all I need, Christophe thought, to go and ask for help from the Courtenays, who hate and despise me...Bah!... They'll really make something of this inheritance story...Everything'll be sorted out... but badly...

His thoughts returned to Murielle, but for some unknown reason, while he was thinking of her in Rome, he only saw a noisy, narrow, grey street, under the rain; he no longer remembered his first sight of Rome, in 1902, when he had visited as a child. He had forgotten that the earth still possessed beautiful landscapes; sun and joy, seemed incomprehensible to him.

He heard midnight sound. What was there left to do? Men and women were coming out of a cinema on the corner of the street. Christophe heard the sound of a voice; a woman shouted some words that got lost in the hubbub, and only the end of her sentence reached his ears:

– To lie down and to sleep, that's the only good...

– What an existence, where during these brief, unique years, accorded to us for living, one only wishes for sleep, to forget it, death, he thought.

He got up with difficulty: sweat ran down his body at the least movement. He crossed the dining room; some large summer roses, wide open like cabbages, distorted by the heat of the night, petals eaten away by rust, were dropping their leaves outside the narrow vase which contained them. Christophe gently lifted the heavy corollas in his hand, which immediately fell back down, went to search for water in the kitchen sink, poured some into the vase, for a second, the perfume from the flowers became stronger, more intoxicating, revived by the drops of water, but almost straight away, the rearranged roses leaned over more, and let their petals fall one by one, which slowly detached themselves with a sort of indifference. Christophe mechanically pushed them away with his feet.

He returned to the kitchen, poured a glass of water, swallowed it in one; it was warm, and smelled slightly of phenol. He went round the two rooms at the back, checking to see that all the shutters were open, in order to let in as much of the night air as possible.

One by one, all along the street, the lights in the windows were going out. A large man with bare arms was still on the doorstep of the house opposite, and was watching the green gas lamp with a dazed expression; it was a clear night, and between the sloping roofs, across the red sky of Paris, distant stars were twinkling in the sky.

Christophe opened the door of his bedroom, sat down on the bed, watched his sleeping wife with the same sustained attention as he had given the flower several moments earlier. She had left a heavy arm hanging outside the sheets, tired hand open. He took it, kept it for a moment in his hands without waking her, then placed it by her side.

– What joy to see her go... I would never leave her, neither for another woman nor to live on my own, he thought again. But if she left first without suffering...

He suddenly realised that he was thinking about her death; he was seized with horror and a superstitious fear. He leant gently toward her, placed his trembling lips on her still forehead. He remembered Murielle's frozen cheek in the shadows of the station two months earlier. " Torn between two women, neither of whom I really love... how weird... But women have never played a very big role in my life..." He thought of Philippe with a confused sadness, then: " I'd be better off asleep... I'm day-dreaming... The heat's overwhelming, he thought. What was she saying, the woman in the street, he thought with a kind of troubled effort, as in a dream, as when memory tries to capture an image from the depths of the past... "To lie down and sleep, that's the only good." Never has a more true word been spoken... I'm thirsty, he thought again."

He poured a second glass, drank the whole lot; the clink of the flask being put back on the table half woke Geneviève; she turned slowly, opened her eyes, looked at Christophe without seeing him, and went back to sleep. A light breath passed between her open lips.

Christophe slid into the bed, pushed back the sheets that stuck to his skin with a feeling of horror.

Not a breath of air. He spent some time looking for a colder place on the pillow, and ended up irritably throwing it on the floor. Somewhere in the house, one o'clock chimed. " I must sleep, he said in an undertone, I'll be fresh tomorrow. Already, I sleep in the office from morning to night. What fear my father successfully installed in them, he thought, so that even with James Bohun dead and buried, they agree to keep me on…"

He mumbled a swearword to himself, angrily opened his pyjama top and threw it on the floor as well, turned over yet again, located the flask and glass with his hand, drank some more.

– I'll never get to sleep, he murmured, with a desperation so disproportionate that he stopped himself, and murmured in an undertone:

– I'm getting hysterical, my word…

He switched on the little bedside lamp and took some books at random. But they only depressed him more…So far from his preoccupations, so distant from his sordid suffering…A detective story had slipped in among them; he read a few pages of it; to lose himself for a minute in the lives of those shadowy beings, involved in a violent action, then he let the book fall, said out loud, gently stressing his words: "I want to be dead." He repeated slowly "dead"… closed his eyes: "What a dream…" The thought of death mysteriously soothed him. " Oh, warmth, warmth… To be lying, naked, on the sand, on a pink beach, in the rising sun…" Two o'clock sounded in the distance.

But he was slowly beginning to lose consciousness, to bury himself in the heavy sleep of those hot Parisian summer nights.

He felt a burning thirst again, but he lacked the energy to stretch out his hand. Suddenly, he seemed to be at the bottom of a small valley, on a very hot afternoon, and a voice that he recognised as his father's, but lighter, like a puff of wind, was remarking in an aside, without addressing him, but just above him:

– The shady valley... Of course, in Nice, let's see, I remember, he said out loud impatiently. A cool delicious green shade, spread out everywhere, surrounded him like deep water. The valley formed two very high walls, covered with leaning trees, high grass, that gently swayed and where the wind blew with a sharp whistle. On the ground, at his feet, he saw a shadowy stretch of water, but perfectly still so that he thought: "I must be dreaming, and this dream is a sign of wellbeing, limpid water means happiness..."

The sun didn't penetrate as far as the water; it had a blackish colour with luminous reflections playing upon it; flowers were growing in profusion, daisies with enormous stalks, that he rushed to gather and make into bunches, without knowing why. And, as soon as he'd done so, they fell apart and dropped from his hands; he felt extraordinary pain and unbounded anger. Finally, he threw them away, and lay down on the ground, at the side of the fast flowing delicious water, and looked up, seeing a colourless sky, in that shade of pearl that sunsets take between high mountains.

Abruptly, as if someone had grabbed him by the shoulder, he woke up. Day was beginning to get going; one could hear the sound of dustbins being picked up and emptied thunderously into parked dustcarts. The lorry began to move, made a shriek, like a superhuman cry, and disappeared.

Christophe got up, yawning.

– What a stupid dream... Only five o'clock, he thought, desperately looking at the time. And it's still very hot... How long can this go on, Lord?...

He got up, walked around the apartment, closed the shutters one by one. The kitchen tiles were already reflecting the bright blue sky, in the narrow funnel-shaped courtyard, linen was drying in every window.

27

Christophe went back into his bedroom, stretched out on the bed, semi-naked, without moving, concentrated on waiting, mindlessly, for the day to break behind the shutters. At seven o'clock, he went into the bathroom, ran cold water into the bath, immersed himself in it with a pleasurable feeling.

There were no shutters in the narrow tiled little room; but a pink and green stained glass window lit up the floor.

Christophe felt better in the freezing bath; the night sweat, a kind of moist pitch that had remained stuck to his limbs, detached itself and ran off him. But as soon as it had gone, as soon as his naked feet touched the baking tiles, and he felt the hot air on his body, he shuddered again, looked anxiously at his face in the mirror.

– What's wrong with me?

Geneviève knocked on the door:

– Coffee's ready Christophe…

He followed her into the dining room, sat silently opposite her.

– If only she'd keep quiet, he thought.

But she began to speak in an unmodulated voice, without looking at him, about Courtenay, about her sister. Perhaps she took some pleasure, some comfort in evoking these familiar childhood figures?...Perhaps the clumsy provocativeness of women, prompted her to speak about things that were "taboo" for him at that minute. He listened to her without saying anything, tensing his lips in a painful little grimace.

Astonished by his silence, she looked at him. He said precipitately:

– When are you going?

– But… after tomorrow…didn't I tell you?...

He murmured:

– Oh, yes… and got up.

She cast her eye over the paper he had dropped, read in an undertone:

– The meteorological office is not predicting any let up in the temperature either today or tomorrow…

– That's good, she murmured, sighing.

Christophe had gone back to get shaved. She began to clear the table dreaming vaguely of the coolness of Courtenay… In her youth, there was a garden behind the house, always dark and a little humid, but in a sunny corner there were espaliers of fruit trees. She closed her eyes, listened in the depths of her memory to the voice of her mother calling: " Henri, Yvonne, Geneviève, take your snack and go and eat it in the orchard…"

Some golden plums were swinging above them.

"Geneviève… Henri… Yvonne…"

She repeated their names in an undertone, with a kind of surprise, thinking of her sister, of her blotchy face, her large sagging cheeks, of her elder brother's grey beard, the one with whom she was going to negotiate the inheritance.

She stopped herself, irritated by the broken sunlight passing through the closed shutters, and by the electric lights coming on, looked at the time.

– Christophe is going to be late, she thought.

Christophe remained still, seated on the side of the bath. Around him, the tiles, the mirror, the running water that sparkled, surrounded him with a kind of flickering flame. The room was narrow and stuffy like a cupboard. The tiles on the walls had taken on a bluish colour; tinted as if washed by the light passing through the windows; the roofs which seemed to climb into the sky were of a violet indigo hue. – The very personification of heat, he thought painfully, that vine colour, violet hillsides under a blazing sky.

He saw his father's dark house again, like a lost paradise, that smell of cloudy mould, the light humidity, the old parquet floors that creaked underfoot... the atmosphere he loved... He had loved the melancholy, the regrets that it awoke in him. He said in an undertone: "...Noble regrets..."

– But this, this brightness, this triumphant mediocrity, how I detest it all, he muttered hatefully. He could already hear the wireless in the next door apartment. The fluctuations of the stock exchange, the market, cotton, corn. Another neighbour used his leisure time in the mornings to study English with a linguaphone. Ten times, twenty-five times, the same slow nasal voice crossed the courtyard: *"What is this? – It is butter. What is this? – It is salt. What is this? – It is bread."*

Above the trellis work that surrounded the kitchen windows, two bare-armed girls were leaning their tousled heads out of the window.

– Amazing heat, one of them, who was young and whose red hair flamed in the sun, cried joyfully: even worse than yesterday!...

And the other, older one, with a large purple congested face and grey streaks in her hair moaned:

It's foul...

Christophe, made an effort to get up, took the razor, dipped it in hot water, then remembered that he hadn't put on shaving cream. The same... Lord... the same routine every morning, every day, until death... he gritted his teeth:

– How many times, he murmured out loud, how many more mornings will I see my head in front of me in this mirror...

Stupidly, he looked at the razor-blade shining in the sun, ran the tips of his fingers across the keen metal.

– That didn't cut, he said softly; he pressed harder and did it again.

– To feel life ebb away, like blood running from open veins in a bath full of hot water, he said in an undertone. At the same time he saw his hot face and dilated eyes in the mirror.

– I'm sick. I'm definitely sick? he murmured. What a head...

He laughed, delicately raised both hands, and his chin, covered with a heavy growth of stubble from the previous night; he spread out his fingers on the skin mechanically, the neck, felt the blue veins, while at the same time looking at his image in the mirror with a kind of scornful interest.

– Let's try, he said.

He took the razor in one hand and drew it across his throat extremely gently, without applying pressure, joyfully saw a thin trickle of scarlet on the skin.

– To cut, to press harder, to feel my head come off, like a ripe fruit…

Suddenly, a nearly involuntary movement, blood ran, stickily through his fingers. But he only felt a slight warmth. He hesitated, half closed his eyes. "I'm mad", he said, and he heard the sound of his far off voice; at the same time a thought went through his mind.

– I'm playing, it's a crazy game, I know I'm going to stop myself. I'm not twenty anymore, look, you don't kill yourself at my age. What nonsense! And why? No, I'm just playing, I press the blade down, I pull it across, I… There you are, he thought all of a sudden, if I hear that odious gramophone again and that voice: "*What is bread?...*" I'm going to press down, and… in a better world, perhaps, he murmured with a stifled laugh.

He waited; the gramophone quietened down, then gently, the mechanism unwound, among the noises, the fracas in the yard, the voices of servants, the creaking of unoiled doors, the clang of dustbins being emptied into waste containers: "*What is this?... It is bread...*" Christophe, in a rage, hit his extended neck with the razor blade, but his hand was trembling. A violent pain went through him. He let himself fall to the ground, saw the pink and green reflections of the stained glass window around him, which was only half open, and on his hands, his naked chest, his white pyjama bottoms, blood was running.

Just at that moment, the door opened. Before half-fainting, he had time to see Geneviève's shocked pale face leaning toward him.

"It's nothing...", he murmured.

– An accident, my poor darling, a silly accident...

Immediately, he closed his eyes, became engulfed by a sort of semi-faint, in which the baking sensation and parching thirst continued, and the feeling of having committed an unspeakable stupidity.

28

Geneviève staunched the blood after some effort. A little water poured on his face brought him back to himself. He was leaning toward Geneviève and his head had fallen back into the crook of her bare arms; he breathed in the soft true scent of lavender which emanated from her, with a strange feeling. Then, he staggered up, moved away from her.

– It's stupid, he said, through clenched teeth: help me to get out of here.

Silently, she supported his arms, while with a supreme effort of all his being, he got up and reached the dining room. There, the blinds and windows were closed; the darkness and the silence soothed him, little by little, the pounding heart that he could feel under his hand, calmed down. All his lucidity came back to him.

– What an idiot! he thought angrily. What took hold of me?

He said in a weak voice:

– I don't know how this ham-fisted accident could have happened… My hand slipped…

– Don't lie. You wanted to kill yourself! she screamed suddenly, in a strange trembling voice that he scarcely recognised... I saw your eyes, your crazy eyes!... But you're mad!... she repeated in a lower voice looking at him in a kind of stupor, it's the act of a madman…

He shrugged his shoulders:

– Listen, you're right. I had a moment of madness. But calm down. It doesn't mean anything…He searched for other words and didn't find them, repeated mechanically:

– doesn't mean anything…

She remained quiet. He added impatiently:

– Give me a drink for the love of God…

In the darkness, he heard her going to get a glass. She came back towards him, brought the glass to his lips, then said softly, in a low trembling voice:

– Is it possible that you loved her that much?

He carefully put the glass back on the table: his fingers trembling.

– What are you talking about? he asked.

She laughed bitterly:

– Oh! Don't try and lie to me. It's not worth it… I've known all about it, and for a long time… That woman, your cousin, she said hatefully, and he noticed that she avoided saying the name Murielle.

He thought, almost happily:

– How they must hate. Perhaps without knowing it…

He passed his hand gently across her face. He needed to speak, reassure, lie… What an effort…

– What a strange idea, he murmured in a weary voice: to think that I would kill myself for a woman…

Yes, it really was a strange idea… yet had he thought of killing himself?... Of course not, a reflex movement…

– Give me a handkerchief, darling…

She shuddered, silently handed him the cloth that was already covered in scarlet stains.

He began softly:

– My poor Geneviève…

But quickly became silent, gave a tired uncaring little sigh. She didn't understand. He, Christophe, to kill himself for woman? Murielle, among a thousand other women… Why Murielle? He saw her face inclined toward the fire once again, with the painful accuracy of dreams, her shoulders enveloped in an old green shawl, leaning forward, heavy with invisible weights. But the familiar image disappeared and other more secret, more treasured ones from the past surged forward. Murielle, with an ardent young face, black hair plaited in a dark crown. He shuddered in spite of himself…all that was long ago…

He remembered Geneviève's words: " I've known all about it, and for a long time…" He looked at her enquiringly:

– What do you think you've known? he asked with mechanical wariness.

– You've always loved her.

He gently raised his eyebrows:

– Always?

– Before our marriage and…

She interrupted herself, turned away and sighed: she hesitated for a moment, no doubt weighing the impact of her dangerous words. She said with an effort:

– At last it's over…

Over. Christophe thought, love… he remembered confusedly the nights they'd gone dancing, returning at dawn in an open car, her young body clasped in his arms. But, of all the images, only one made him shudder with regret, the woods at Ville-d'Avray and the cold lake in the early morning, the wind blowing in their faces, pure, and charged with acrid vegetable scents...

He said irritably and with a bitter, sardonic tone that surprised himself:

– Decidedly, women are crazy.

He thought:

– Now she's going to ask if I still love her. God! he murmured clenching his teeth, I just want some peace!

But Geneviève didn't ask anything. She opened the kitchen door and began to wash the breakfast cups. She didn't know how to be inactive; her hands were clever and agile, and their movement soothed her, got on top of her fever.

Christophe got up with a sigh, looked at the time.

– I'm not going into the office today. I'm going back to bed. What train are you taking the day after tomorrow? She hesitated for an instant, then replied in a low voice:

– But I... I don't know... in any case I'm not leaving the day after tomorrow...

– Why? he shouted in a fit of blind rage.

She had adopted that serene, inhuman tone of voice, which he hated, the one she used to calm Philippe as a child.

– You're nervy. You're sick. It'll be better if I stay.

He mastered himself with a violent effort, squeezed his trembling hands against each other.

– Don't ever speak to me again about this absurd thing and don't speak about Murielle. That... that'll be better believe me... I repeat, I had a moment of madness. It happens. I held that blade in my hands, and, all of a sudden, I closed my eyes and I pressed down. It was a completely clumsy movement, unconscious if you prefer. Does one kill oneself at the age of forty-three, and for love? he finished with a weary little laugh.

Without waiting for her response, he went towards the door; he wanted nothing other than to bury himself in a vast fresh bed; the closed shutters would stop the shouts and heat of the street from coming in. His neck was aching.

– What idiocy, he murmured angrily one last time, and, falling on the bed, feeling the unmade sheets between his legs, with a deep sigh, he went to sleep.

Geneviève closed the door behind him, sat down on the first empty chair, watching the low dark room with hostility, as if it were an alien bedroom. She felt a shiver, a cry of revolt:

– And me? He never thinks of me?

Had he truly thought to kill himself? That was so unlike him. But what do I know about him? she thought, sadly. He was a being from another race, the son of James Bohun, who dies without a word of complaint, without a call for pity, with his eternal weary little grimacing smile, flitting on the corners of his breathless lips, already dried by death.

She sighed, mentally addressing an invisible interlocutor.

– How difficult he is to understand…

She shed some tears, then desperately regained his memory, his image.

– Oh! my God, I'm tired, me too… It'll be better if I go. He'll be calmer. I tire him, she thought with bitter humility: Philippe as well, is always tired and irrita... Oh! my God. I'm too old to be happy and too young to have stopped suffering. Courtenay, the freshness in the garden...

The weighty atmosphere in the room seemed to fall back more heavily on her shoulders. She slowly wiped the tears that were forming in the corners of her eyes, which had run down to her lips; she drank them with a desolate languor, and, gently, back bent forward, she went to open the door for the housekeeper.

29

During the evening, Christophe, comforted by several hours of dreamless sleep, managed to find the necessary words to permit his wife to leave without bad conscience.

He dilated at length on the accident, recounted in an ironic and nonchalant tone how he'd thought: "If I hear that linguaphone one more time…"

She listened silently, eyes lowered, thinking: "Doubtless he's telling the truth…"

– First thing tomorrow morning, Christophe continued, I'm going to see a doctor. I must be terribly down and depressed. He'll give me some kind of tranquilliser.

– That's sensible.

– If you like it at Courtenay, write to me. I'll come and ask you for a weekend's hospitality, he added, after a sudden inspiration.

Geneviève blushed lightly, murmured with an expression of pleasure:

– That's a good idea.

So in the evening of the day after the following day, she left.

He accompanied her to the station; it was late, nearly midnight; the last local trains were stopping at the platforms, the crowd moved slowly out of the carriages; women stumbling, crushed by the double weight of sleeping children and enormous bunches of wild flowers, already half opened, that they were carrying in their arms.

The train carrying Geneviève left. An odd sense of wellbeing spread though Christophe. On leaving the station he breathed in the hot air with delight.

He hailed a taxi automatically, climbed in, thought too late that he should have taken the metro, then shrugged his shoulders. He felt weary; his head felt strangely dizzy.

It was a tropical night. The heavens seemed moist and sticky like pitch. He leaned his forehead back, looked between the roofs at the stars, scarcely visible, flickering slightly. He opened his mouth wide, hoping for some fresher air to breathe, but even the movement of the car failed to cause a puff of wind. They passed under some chestnut trees, lit from below by arc lamps; their leaves weren't moving; they were already pink and dry as in autumn. The dust had the taste of roasted almonds; it stung the eyes...

– Murielle... What's the good? What's the good? He looked hatefully at the cars packed with cases that went past. To feel a racing car under his hand, fast and silent...

– My only wish, the fastest car in France!...

Once again he threw his head back, drank in the fiery air, which smelt of dust and petrol. Some men without jackets, others in white tennis shirts with open necks were sitting in the street cafes; women in light sleeveless dresses went past slowly, abruptly spreading their arms as if swimming, to rid themselves of the sticky sensation of material on their skin. Christophe noticed perfunctorily that the heat didn't stop them from having fur stoles, but most couldn't be bothered to put them round their shoulders; they held them by the ends of the paws, like dead rabbits, and gently swung them. Everybody walked slowly, stopping from time to time to wipe the sweat running down their foreheads; all these faces suddenly illuminated by headlamps in the street, that came and went with passing cars, creating a mysterious atmosphere. "Some living mirrors", Christophe thought.

He got out at Weber's, sat down at a table outside, opened his mouth to order a martini, then economic worries came back to him; a beer would do. He drank it; the beer went to his head even more. He lit a cigarette, breathed in the smoke greedily. The bus from the Madelaine to the Concorde went by in front of him, nearly brushed the side of his table, which was the outermost on the pavement; they seemed to be rushing at an insane speed; and the traffic lights that lit up the road, alternately red and green, were turning in front of his eyes. His blood was beating in his temples, blasts of hot air buffeted his eyelids. The sky itself, like a raging torrent, seemed to flow angrily above him. He closed his eyes, desperate for peace and silence.

– I'm tired... And without doubt there must be more in the world than money and leisure... I'm lazy, I'm asking for paradise, basically, I'm reclaiming paradise, I reject, I hate, I abominate God's commandment: "With the sweat of thy brow..." Life... Isn't it odious to accord such importance to the material side of life? But if one takes away all that, what's left, I ask you, he murmured, feverishly addressing an invisible interlocutor. If one takes away soft, comfortably fitting clothes, beautifully cold bed-linen, crockery, fine wines served in beautiful glasses, idleness, leisure, what's left? Yes... yes... I know perfectly well, thoughts, love... But for that you need a free heart and mind... and I'm enslaved until the end of my days... God!... I'm hot, he murmured once again, and he looked around stupefied. The absurd little cut, rubbed on by his shirt collar, was hurting him more all the time. But he didn't want to think about that idiotic pain, which reminded him, moment by moment of that brief madness of which he was ashamed. Abruptly, he thought of his father, with a feeling of envy, in the little cemetery, where the summer flowers bloomed. He had brought roses there, the night before... It was the only place in Paris one could breathe; there was always a fresh light wind blowing, a delicious humidity rose up from the constantly watered ground, and the trees were taller and thicker than anywhere else... How much time would go by before, he too, would be lying there?... He didn't fear death, nor the immobility, the silence, this cold deep earth... How desirable that seemed in a heat like this, the scented earth, traversed by roots and swollen with sap... What was hateable, were the masonry tombs, so heavy, without doubt, and the wood, the iron on the casket, the clothing... He closed his eyes and dreamed of sleep, naked, in the earth, the earth biting into his bones and penetrating his flesh...To dissolve, to disappear quickly, to become mere matter..., to feel crossed only by swirling waves of hot and cold... The pavement underfoot was melting in the baking air...Death...He sighed. He was still young and healthy. Peace was good for others... For him...How he envied those who despaired for reasons of love, feelings...There were some still, perhaps...To be cheated on, for example!... There were still people who suffered because a woman cheated on them... Comical...It was rare, it's true... But it happened sometimes... He remembered Geneviève. " She loves me, she's jealous, she's left me, however, with a feeling of deliverance... But no, it's no longer love... She's... deceiving herself, he thought abruptly and he laughed with effort, feeling an intolerable burning spread from his neck through his whole body... And the other one too, Murielle... She loves her youth, in me, it's past... Ah! I understand them all too well, and myself."

He stood up painfully, hailed a taxi that was cruising slowly by.

And immediately he forgot the women. The taxi drove rapidly along the deserted quays. Christophe leaned his face on the car door, watched the reflection of the lamps in the water, flicker and fade. Useless life, life more worthless than that of a dog...And millions of beings live like that?...Surrounded by millions who aspire to this life, as the unique good accorded to man?...

He laughed. He thought:

– That's a proud notion of man... Who said that?...

He made a stupendous effort to remember, but couldn't. He made a sign with his hand, said to the driver in a weary tone:

– Faster… would you?... drive faster?...

The Seine was the most beautiful thing in the world… Strange lights, some spilled heaps of coal, the open entrance of a little red bistro, from which a violent song escaped… Morning was coming. A fresh wind put a flavour a new purity into the air.

30

The next day he woke up late. He had slept badly
half the night and in the morning dreamt of wind, a
storm. On opening his eyes he noticed that the open
door must have been knocking during his sleep, and
that was the cause of the strange groaning, howling
noise, which still filled his ears. He drew the blinds,
looked avidly for a sign of rain in the sky, but the
brutal light of the sun entered his eyes like a jet of
flame. He threw a tired glance at the roofs opposite.
Under the sky darkened by the storm which had
covered Paris for weeks and never burst, their dry
violet colour was even more pronounced.

He closed up the shutters sighing, turned around,
hearing the noise of footsteps in the dining room;
the housekeeper was there, a Madame Victoire in a
grey pinafore, with a purplish face congested by the
heat, and a crown of tousled white hair.

Christophe looked at her, asked:

– The kids are in the country?

She seemed surprised, but said with a rapturous
expression:

– Oh yes, monsieur!

He had guessed correctly that she was one of
those creatures whose husband or children,
according to the situation, seem to be enjoying
themselves, while they themselves stay labouring
away in the obscure depths. And she was happy
with it. He thought with a profound sadness:

– Only an excess of love can help to bear this
life, but love isn't given to everyone.

He spoke with a gentleness that astonished even himself, without irony, neither in his heart nor on his lips, but with interest and a vague sympathy;

– As long as they're happy, that's the main thing…

The woman sighed:

– Yes, Monsieur

And:

– Monsieur also has a grown up son?

– Of course, Christophe said. He thought of his son, shrugged his shoulders. He couldn't even console himself with the same words…Philippe wasn't happy… Philippe was just as unstable and unhappy as he himself was…

He went to get dressed, looked with astonishment at the way the little wound from the previous night appeared. His whole neck was red and swollen. He swore, began to look for an antiseptic stick, without success, he turned the little medicine cabinet on the wall upside down. He found a bottle of iodine, but it was empty, it only contained a little brown tincture stuck to the bottom of the bottle.

Just at that moment, Victoire knocked at the door.

– Nine o'clock…

He was going to be late once again. He had already missed the office yesterday morning… Moreover he had sworn to take buses rather than taxis from now on. " I haven't time."

He threw away the empty bottle impatiently, followed the old lady into the dining room. Standing up and finishing dressing at the same time, he swallowed a cup of coffee. He was tired and ill at ease; the pain in his neck got worse with every movement.

But he forced himself to think of something else. He put back his cup with an effort, threw the paper which he hadn't read to the ground, and left.

Outside, it seemed like entering a steam bath. The tarmac was melting. The air was heavy and viscous; he spread out his arms instinctively like a swimmer ploughing through water.

He went up to his office and began his habitual work.

Two hours later, when the pain had become intolerable, accompanied by a sensation of nausea and sudden rigors that shook his whole body, one of the typists, astonished by his rough, hoarse, breathless voice, looked toward him.

– Monsieur Bohun, what's the matter? Are you ill?

He passed his hand slowly across his forehead.

– It's the heat, no doubt, he murmured. Why are you looking at me like that? What's wrong with me?

She handed him a little mirror; he looked carefully at the swollen purple face with dilated eyes, burning with fever. He made an effort to point out his wound:

– It's that… that thing, that little cut I've got on my neck, I don't know how, I was shaving, it must be infected…

– Wait, said the typist briskly.

She went out, and came back with a bottle of iodine, painted the bottom of his cheeks and neck with it. He let himself go for a moment; his head was bursting, and purple-tinted concentric rings and circles, the colour of fresh blood, were passing in front of his eyes.

But the heat given off by the typist's body, the contact with her naked arms, the smell of her armpits, visible under her muslin blouse, made his heart pound. He pushed her lightly, murmuring impatiently:

But it's nothing at all, look my little darling, thanks very much, it'll be OK now. I'll see to it when I get home.

He went back to dictating letters. After a while, he had to stop for a second time. His cheeks were on fire and strange shivers were running down his back; like icy snakes, they slithered with extreme speed from neck to kidney. He closed his eyes, said angrily:

– Too bad, I'm going home.

Midday sounded somewhere. When he saw the steak on his table, carefully prepared by Madame Victoire, who had gone, her work having finished; a bitter bile left his lips. He took fright, called his wife, but she was far away. He dragged himself as far as the caretaker's lodge, seized the telephone receiver and randomly called one doctor after another. Vacancies... vacancies... Every time there was just an answering service replying in a monotonous voice:

" The subscriber is away from Paris until September."

He went back to his own apartment to get some money, to drive to the first chemist's shop he came to.

– Blood poisoning, probably, he thought with an effort. But how tired I am…

He sat on the edge of the bed for a moment, to let the heavy irregular beating of his heart calm down. But his head began to turn, slowly; he closed his eyes, engulfed in a kind of semi-faint.

When he came out of it, when he was able to escape from the soft exhausting stickiness, the bedroom was dark; a single long golden arrow of dust crossed the room from the window to the copper ball on the bedpost.

All he could see was this golden ball glittering in the shadows; its dazzling flashes penetrated his eyes and entered his sick brain, piercing one place then another, like poisoned needles. Poisoned… he repeated it out loud several times with a sort of astonishment, understood at last. The fever throbbed inside him, shook him, threw him against the bars of the bed which he automatically clutched and pushed away. But his mind remained cynical and lucid. This was, if not better, at least as good as… He was sick of life, for a long time he'd been sick of life. It had given him a few beautiful years. No! Some beautiful days. The tally was quickly made. Not childhood. Perhaps that ball game in the sun in a London garden blooming with flowers? A pink beach in autumn, in the depths of his dreams, in the depths of time… When he retrieved that image he shivered with desire. There was only one good thing, to lie in the sun, or in light shade, with the soft deep sound of the sea. But, he would have all that. He would be lying in an eternal, gentle, coolness, and the movement of bursting seeds, the shivering of the earth, the warm winds, the long roots, twisted like snakes at the bottom of a hole, the vegetable scent that he loved so much... all that, would be his eter... eternally...

" For beings like me, who haven't loved their lives, those to whom the earth was allotted. God would perhaps allow them, to be transformed into animals, plants, minerals, stones, who knows?... Eternally."

A green light was burning in his head and shifted from one side to the other. What was there left to regret? The woman? The devil take it... He'd forgotten her name... That woman who rose up out of his past, with her black tresses of hair, falling around her pale face?

– It's strange that at the moment of death, I can scarcely remember the looks or the name of the one I loved... the only woman in the world, on earth, in life, that I loved... My short, my only life. I couldn't give a damn. It was a long time ago, the whole lot's gone. One dies at the age of twenty. One dies when there's no more joy. Damned life... Incomprehensible... I didn't know how to live, perhaps, perhaps... but with all my heart I consent to die...That's also important...

He woke up completely and saw that night had fallen. Flies were buzzing about. In the distance a gramophone was playing, and the stifled husky sound suddenly brought back Murielle's voice and her face, and all the scents of this terrestrial life running from him, "like blood escaping slowly from cut veins…" He felt pain for a moment. He, who for years, had only ever felt anger and a sort of repressed savage bitterness, he felt his own pain. He looked at his hands with tenderness, his beautiful hands, which were gradually becoming purple under the nails and which would soon be motionless under the earth… But what do you know, it was better than living like this. He thought again of Geneviève, of Philippe… or, at least, the thought crossed his mind that he didn't want to see them again, that they had stayed very far away, on the surface, while he was engulfed, being dragged down into the black depths. He murmured: " My wife… my son…" laughed, pushed his lips forward, with a savage movement, that grinding grimace that belonged to him, and the effort cut short his breath. His arms involuntarily stiffened, he spread them out abruptly, looked at the copper ball that a flash of moonlight caused to flicker and twinkle in the shadows; he exhaled a long peaceful sigh, threw back his head, suffocated for a single second and managed to die.

Manufactured by Amazon.ca
Bolton, ON